FROM THE
NANCY DREW FILES

THE CASE: A desperate late-night call for help draws Nancy into a deadly race against time.

CONTACT: The hotline caller is a girl on the run from a killer who may already have her number.

SUSPECTS: Kip DiFranco—*Paul Remer, the dead guy, once belonged to Kip's street gang—until Paul turned on him and turned him in to the police.*

Billie Peters—*Kip's girlfriend, she's as tough as they come, and she'd do anything to protect him.*

Helen Tremain Thackett—*Rachel's mother, she wanted Paul Remer out of her daughter's life . . . no matter how high the price.*

COMPLICATIONS: Nancy has no hope of finding the murderer unless she can first find the one reliable witness—who may soon become the next victim!

Books in The Nancy Drew Files® Series

#1	SECRETS CAN KILL	#47	FLIRTING WITH DANGER
#2	DEADLY INTENT	#48	A DATE WITH DECEPTION
#3	MURDER ON ICE	#49	PORTRAIT IN CRIME
#4	SMILE AND SAY MURDER	#50	DEEP SECRETS
#5	HIT AND RUN HOLIDAY	#51	A MODEL CRIME
#6	WHITE WATER TERROR	#52	DANGER FOR HIRE
#7	DEADLY DOUBLES	#53	TRAIL OF LIES
#8	TWO POINTS TO MURDER	#54	COLD AS ICE
#9	FALSE MOVES	#55	DON'T LOOK TWICE
#10	BURIED SECRETS	#56	MAKE NO MISTAKE
#11	HEART OF DANGER	#57	INTO THIN AIR
#12	FATAL RANSOM	#58	HOT PURSUIT
#13	WINGS OF FEAR	#59	HIGH RISK
#14	THIS SIDE OF EVIL	#60	POISON PEN
#15	TRIAL BY FIRE	#61	SWEET REVENGE
#16	NEVER SAY DIE	#62	EASY MARKS
#17	STAY TUNED FOR DANGER	#63	MIXED SIGNALS
		#64	THE WRONG TRACK
#18	CIRCLE OF EVIL	#65	FINAL NOTES
#19	SISTERS IN CRIME	#66	TALL, DARK AND DEADLY
#20	VERY DEADLY YOURS		
#21	RECIPE FOR MURDER	#67	NOBODY'S BUSINESS
#22	FATAL ATTRACTION	#68	CROSSCURRENTS
#23	SINISTER PARADISE	#69	RUNNING SCARED
#24	TILL DEATH DO US PART	#70	CUTTING EDGE
#25	RICH AND DANGEROUS	#71	HOT TRACKS
#26	PLAYING WITH FIRE	#72	SWISS SECRETS
#27	MOST LIKELY TO DIE	#73	RENDEZVOUS IN ROME
#28	THE BLACK WIDOW	#74	GREEK ODYSSEY
#29	PURE POISON	#75	A TALENT FOR MURDER
#30	DEATH BY DESIGN	#76	THE PERFECT PLOT
#31	TROUBLE IN TAHITI	#77	DANGER ON PARADE
#32	HIGH MARKS FOR MALICE	#78	UPDATE ON CRIME
		#79	NO LAUGHING MATTER
#33	DANGER IN DISGUISE	#80	POWER OF SUGGESTION
#34	VANISHING ACT	#81	MAKING WAVES
#35	BAD MEDICINE	#82	DANGEROUS RELATIONS
#36	OVER THE EDGE	#83	DIAMOND DECEIT
#37	LAST DANCE	#84	CHOOSING SIDES
#38	THE FINAL SCENE	#85	SEA OF SUSPICION
#39	THE SUSPECT NEXT DOOR	#86	LET'S TALK TERROR
		#87	MOVING TARGET
#40	SHADOW OF A DOUBT	#88	FALSE PRETENSES
#41	SOMETHING TO HIDE	#89	DESIGNS IN CRIME
#42	THE WRONG CHEMISTRY	#90	STAGE FRIGHT
#43	FALSE IMPRESSIONS	#91	IF LOOKS COULD KILL
#44	SCENT OF DANGER	#92	MY DEADLY VALENTINE
#45	OUT OF BOUNDS	#93	HOTLINE TO DANGER
#46	WIN, PLACE OR DIE		

Available from ARCHWAY Paperbacks

The Nancy Drew Files ™

Case 93
Hotline to Danger
Carolyn Keene

AN ARCHWAY PAPERBACK
Published by POCKET BOOKS

New York   London   Toronto   Sydney   Tokyo   Singapore

AN ARCHWAY PAPERBACK *Original*

An Archway Paperback published by
POCKET BOOKS, a division of Simon & Schuster Inc.
1230 Avenue of the Americas, New York, NY 10020

Copyright © 1994 Simon & Schuster Inc.
Produced by Mega-Books of New York, Inc.

ISBN: 0-671-79485-X

First Archway Paperback printing March 1994

10 9 8 7 6 5 4 3 2 1

NANCY DREW, AN ARCHWAY PAPERBACK and colophon are registered trademarks of Simon & Schuster Inc.

THE NANCY DREW FILES is a trademark of Simon & Schuster Inc.

Cover art by Cliff Miller

Printed in the U.S.A.

IL 6+

Hotline to Danger

Chapter

One

"HELLO, HELP IS HERE HOTLINE. This is Nancy. How can I help you?" Nancy Drew said into the telephone receiver. She was seated at an old desk in a drab, sparsely furnished room on the second floor of the River Heights Teen Center.

On the other side of the desk, her good friends Bess Marvin and George Fayne watched her. Bess was perched on the edge of the desk. Her cousin George was leaning forward in her chair, her intense, dark eyes riveted on Nancy.

It was the first call that had come in during the girls' volunteer shift at the teen center's hotline. The three had spent six weeks training at the center, so they knew how important it was to be a good listener and refer the callers to a professional for help, if necessary.

1

Flipping back her reddish blond hair, Nancy switched the phone to her other ear. "Uh-huh. And you're feeling hurt because your friend is seeing so much of this guy?"

She glanced down at the information sheet in front of her on the desk. Callers didn't have to give their names, but the volunteers had to write down the times of all calls and what they were about. Nancy glanced at her watch, then wrote down the time. "Jealous? No. I can understand that," Nancy said. "It's tough to lose a best friend. And it sounds like the two of you were incredibly close before this guy came along."

George and Bess smiled at each other. Behind them, tall, raven-haired Tony Ramirez, the hotline coordinator, was listening, too. Tony was a graduate student in psychology. He coordinated the hotline and counseling programs at the teen center. Even though he was twenty-three, in his faded jeans and a sweatshirt with the sleeves cut off at the elbows, Tony could have passed for one of the many teens who hung out at the center.

"That's an idea. You could talk to her and tell her how you feel," Nancy said. Her gaze settled on the list of referral groups and professionals taped on the desk beside the phone. "But, you know, the high school has a great peer program," she told the girl on the other end of the line. "What about talking to them?"

Nancy smiled when the caller said she thought that was a good idea. "We'll be here until eleven," she assured the girl. "So if you're feeling down, don't hesitate to call again. Okay? 'Bye."

"Whew!" Nancy sighed in relief as she hung up the phone. Quickly she jotted down the nature of the call. "I didn't think helping someone could be so tough."

"Only you made it sound easy," George said.

"Really. Congratulations, Nan," Bess said, jumping off the desk. "You did everything Tony taught us to do in the training sessions."

"Right," Tony agreed. "Especially the part about being a good listener. Remember, our job isn't to solve the callers' problems. It's to listen and refer them to someone who can help."

"I hope I can do as well as you," Bess said, running her fingers through her long, blond hair.

Watching her friend, Nancy thought how good Bess looked in her short black skirt, black knit leggings, and red sweater. She herself had opted for jeans and a sweatshirt, as had George. But ever since Bess had started dating Kyle Donovan, she had been dressing and looking even better than usual.

Just then the shrill jangle of the telephone made Nancy jump. For a second, all three girls stared at the phone.

Then Bess reached for the receiver. "My turn." She took a deep breath, then picked it up. "Hello. Help Is Here Hotline. This is Bess."

Nancy saw the anxiousness in Bess's eyes and gave her friend the thumbs-up sign. Soon Bess was nodding her head earnestly as she listened to the caller.

"It's all right to cry," Bess finally said, tears welling in her own eyes. "I'd cry too if my boyfriend was moving away." As she listened, Bess reached into the desk drawer for a tissue and blew her nose.

Grinning, Tony shook his head. "I think you could say Bess is a little too involved with her work," he whispered.

Two phones had been installed for the hotline, and just then the second phone rang. George raced over to the other desk to get the call.

"Sounds like you three are going to be busy tonight," Tony said to Nancy. The hotline was open every morning, late afternoon, and evening. From twelve to three it was closed. Once Tony had enough volunteers, the hotline would be open from nine in the morning until eleven at night. "Obviously, I need only two people to answer phones. But I'm glad all three of you could be here for your first night. Since I'll be around, I can answer any questions that come up."

Bess said goodbye and hung up the phone. "Oh, boy," she said. "That was a tough one." She shook her head as she wrote down several notes on the information sheet. "The girl who called is named Clarise, and her boyfriend's moving to Ohio. He's a junior. She wants him to stay here until he graduates, but his parents won't let him.

One top of that, *her* mom can't stand the guy and is always bad-mouthing him. She's really down about the whole thing."

"You handled it well, Bess," Tony said. "The callers want a sympathetic listener, not someone who judges or just tries to cheer them up. But remember—you've got to keep some distance. You can't get too involved with the caller. It doesn't help them *or* you."

"Whew." George dropped the receiver into its cradle a moment later and ran a hand through her curly brown hair. "That caller has some heavy-duty problems at school. I think I convinced him to make an appointment to see you, Tony."

The hotline coordinator nodded. "Good work. But remember, you can only suggest that they get help. The caller is the one who has to follow through because he or she *wants* to."

"Right," Nancy, Bess, and George chorused. They had learned all this during training, but it was good to hear it again now that they were confronted with real callers who had real problems.

"How about if I treat you guys to sodas," Tony suggested. "It's going to be a long night."

"Sounds like a good idea," Bess said. "I'll go down to the machine with you and help bring them back."

The two of them were headed for the door when Bess's boyfriend, Kyle Donovan, walked in. With his curly blond hair, blue eyes, sharp cheekbones, and cleft chin, he looked like a model in a men's magazine, Nancy thought.

"Kyle!" Bess said in a surprised voice. "What are you doing here?"

"Coming to see you," he replied. "Since you've been spending all your time at the hotline, I've almost forgotten what you look like." He unzipped his bomber jacket.

Bess opened her mouth to reply when both phones rang.

"Busy is right," George said as she and Nancy dove for the phones.

"Help Is Here Hotline," Nancy repeated. A guy's voice greeted her heartily on the other end. But the longer Nancy listened, the more she suspected the cheerfulness was put on. The caller actually sounded lonely and depressed.

While Nancy listened, she watched Bess introduce Kyle to Tony. Then Tony left to get the sodas, and Bess and Kyle sauntered into the hall.

"My parents are getting divorced," the caller finally said, his voice filled with emotion. "I mean, this is my senior year! How can they do this to me?"

"You sound really mad at them," Nancy said, trying to echo the caller's feelings.

The guy snorted. "You're not kidding. I'm so mad I could—" A sob cut off his words. Nancy remained silent. She knew that her job was to listen, even if all the caller wanted to do was cry.

Abruptly, he started talking again, some of the cockiness back in his voice. "Well, I guess lots of parents get divorced these days. So it's no big deal." He stopped, as if waiting for Nancy to respond.

She kept quiet a moment, then said, "There *are* a lot of parents getting divorced. You know, the center has a group for teens whose parents are separating or divorcing." She gave him the time it met.

"No way." The caller laughed. "Probably a bunch of crybabies join it."

"Well, you'll never know unless you come. Right?" Nancy kept her voice light.

"Right. Anyway, thanks," the caller said.

Tony came back into the room and set a soft drink can on the desk in front of George, then a can in front of Nancy just as the caller hung up. "You look like you could use this."

Nancy exhaled with a sigh as she reached for the soft drink. "That's for sure. Maybe I'm not cut out for this. It's hard just listening. I want to give them advice!"

"I know," Tony said. "It's hard sometimes to just listen. But that's what the callers need." He sat on the edge of the desk. George was still talking to her caller.

"Okay, guys. It's my turn," Bess said as she came back into the room. Her cheeks were flushed, but her expression was solemn.

Nancy raised one brow. "Did Kyle leave?"

7

Bess nodded. "Yeah. He's really excited. He's been accepted to law school."

"That's great! Kyle's been working as a paralegal at my father's firm," Nancy explained to Tony. "Where's he going? Chicago?"

Bess sighed, and her shoulders slumped. "Chicago would be great. At least he'd be close. But he's been accepted by a school in California, and, well—" She glanced wistfully at Nancy. "You know how hard long-distance romances are."

Nancy nodded, her thoughts straying to her own boyfriend, Ned Nickerson, who was a student at Emerson College.

"Cheer up, Bess," Tony said. "A great-looking girl like you could have tons of dates if you wanted. Besides, you're too young to get serious with one guy."

"Oh, really?" Bess tilted her head and gazed up at him from under her lashes. "Is that advice from Tony the psychologist?"

Tony chuckled. "Uh, no. That's advice from Tony the guy."

Uh-oh, Nancy thought as Tony and Bess gazed at each other. She could almost feel the vibes between them. Not that she could blame Bess. Tony was a great guy, and Bess loved to flirt. But ever since Bess had been dating Kyle, she'd been pretty serious about their relationship.

Just then George hung up the phone and spun around in her seat to face the others.

"How'd it go?" Tony asked.

"Not good," George said, opening her soda can. "It was a girl calling about her younger sister, who's kind of the family favorite. The girl said she loves her sister but that sometimes she feels neglected. I just wish she hadn't hung up so soon. If she'd only talked a little longer, I think she would have felt better."

George's phone rang again, and this time Bess grabbed it. Then the phone next to Nancy rang. She reached for the receiver.

"Help Is Here Hotline. This is Nancy." She paused, waiting for the caller to respond. But there was silence, as if no one was on the line.

Then Nancy heard sobbing. Someone *was* there, she realized. Someone who needed help. "Hi. Would you like to talk?"

Pausing again, Nancy counted slowly to ten. Don't rush the caller, she told herself. It was one of Tony's most important rules.

"I—" a faint voice stammered on the other end. "I need to—"

The caller stopped, but Nancy could tell that it was a girl.

"If you tell me what's on your mind, maybe I can help," Nancy said in a soothing voice.

"I want to. But I can't now. . . ." The voice trailed off.

"Hey. If it's too hard to talk now, we'll be here until eleven," Nancy continued. "Or you can call tomorrow."

There was a ragged intake of breath, then

steadier breathing, as if the caller was trying to get hold of herself. Nancy's mind raced back through her training sessions. What should she say to convince the girl it was all right to talk?

"Or I can just stay on the line until you're ready," Nancy said calmly. "That's what I'm here for."

But the caller only began to sob again. Then in a shrill voice, she cried, "Fourteenth. Tracks. I can't tell you any more!"

"Wait! At least tell me if you're all right!" Nancy exclaimed.

But the caller didn't answer.

The line went dead.

Chapter

Two

As she lowered the receiver, Nancy stared silently at the mouthpiece. She couldn't believe the caller had hung up. From the sound of the girl's voice, she was in big trouble. And Nancy had lost her!

"Nan? Are you all right?"

George's voice made Nancy look up. Both George and Tony were watching her.

"She hung up," Nancy said, looking distressed.

Tony reached out and squeezed Nancy's shoulder. "That happens sometimes, my friend. Maybe she'll call back when she's ready to talk."

Pushing back the desk chair, Nancy said, "I don't think so. It sounded like she was in trouble."

She stood up and walked to the room's front windows. They looked out on Main Street in the old part of River Heights. The teen center occupied a three-story building that had once been a small department store. The hotline was in a room on the second floor.

Below, a few streetlamps illuminated the sidewalks and storefronts. The old end of Main Street was gradually being renovated. Many trendy shops and restaurants had already moved in, and the historic buildings were getting facelifts.

"What do you mean she was in trouble?" Tony asked.

"I think Nancy smells a mystery," George said.

"No," Tony said. "It's no mystery. I warned you about the callers who talk for a second, then panic and hang up."

"Only this caller was trying to tell me something," Nancy said, whipping around to face the others. "She gave me two clues—'fourteenth' and 'tracks.'" She strode over to the desk. "Fourteenth. That either means a date—"

"Or a street," Bess added excitedly, having heard the end of the conversation after her own caller had hung up. "But what does 'tracks' mean?"

"It could mean footprints or—" Nancy paused. "Railroad tracks? Maybe something happened to our caller at the railroad tracks near Fourteenth Street?"

"Wait a minute." Tony raised one hand. "This

is a hotline, not a detective agency. We don't get involved with the callers."

"Unless someone's in trouble," Nancy said, glancing sharply at Tony. "Look, you know I'm a detective. I won't do anything while I'm working at the hotline, but my instincts tell me that I need to check out the caller's message. Remember, if someone's in real danger it *is* our responsibility to make sure they get help."

Tony nodded. "You're right. Only I'm coming with you."

Just then the hotline phone rang, and George reached for it. Nancy checked her watch. It was ten-fifteen. As soon as they closed up for the night, she was going to check out the caller's clues. She had a hunch they were a cry for help.

"Fourteenth Street isn't far from here," Nancy said as she, Bess, George, and Tony got ready to leave the hotline office forty-five minutes later. They had turned on the answering machine, which gave late-night callers a number they could dial for emergency help.

"It's in a rough part of town, though," George noted as she slipped on her jacket.

"That's one reason I'm going with you," Tony said as the teens headed for the door.

The four of them clattered down the wooden steps of the teen center. On the first floor were a meeting room, a recreation hall, and a small office for the director, Arnold Rosensteel. Mr. A,

13

the nickname the teens had given Mr. Rosensteel, had started the center about five years earlier. He'd taken the rundown store and slowly turned it into a safe haven for runaways, dropouts, and kids who had no place else to hang out.

The hotline had been started only recently. When Nancy, Bess, and George had heard about it from friends, they decided to take the training course.

All during the evening shift, the first floor of the center had been filled with the sounds of teens talking, laughing, and playing video games. Now it was quiet, since the center itself closed at ten-thirty.

Nancy had never been up to the third floor, but Tony had told her that Mr. A was turning it into a dorm where runaways could stay until they found permanent accommodations.

"Let me tell Mr. A we're leaving," Tony said when they reached the front foyer. He strode down the hall toward the director's office.

Nancy caught a glimpse of the director's bald head as Tony opened the office door. She knew that Mr. A often stayed late. The center was a success because of all his hard work.

A minute later Tony came out of the office, his jacket draped over one shoulder. "All set," he said, putting on his jacket. He held open the front door, and they all filed outside. It was a chilly March night, and Nancy zipped up her down jacket against the brisk air.

"So you really think that 'fourteenth' means a street?" George asked as she got into the backseat of Nancy's Mustang with Bess. Tony settled his long frame in the front seat, then shut the car door.

"It makes sense." Nancy started the car and pulled away from the curb. "Fourteenth Street leads to the industrial section of town. There are a lot of warehouses, and behind the ones on the south side of the street are some old railroad tracks."

"Hey, Nan," Bess said from the backseat. "Isn't that where we found my Camaro when it was stolen?"

Nancy nodded. "Yes. The chop shop was on Tenth Street."

She turned down Fourteenth Street. Several streetlights shone down on rusty chain-link fences and trash-filled curbs. Some of the warehouses that flanked the street were boarded up. Others had broken windows.

"Boy, this place doesn't look too prosperous," George said.

"It used to be," Tony commented. "But when the new highway went in, business moved out to the suburbs."

Nancy slowed the car. "The tracks run behind this block of warehouses."

"Oh, boy," Bess muttered. "That's a lot of territory to cover, considering we don't know what we're looking for."

"Hey. Isn't that a phone booth up ahead?" Nancy asked, squinting as she looked through the windshield.

"Yeah. I think it is," George replied.

Nancy drove toward the glass booth. "Maybe that's where the caller phoned from," Nancy said. After parking in front of the booth, Nancy jumped out. When she opened the glass door, she noticed that the receiver was dangling off the hook. Nancy picked it up, then jiggled the hook. The phone still worked.

"Look!" Bess exclaimed, coming up to Nancy. George and Tony were right behind her. Bending down, Bess pointed at an embroidered bracelet lying on the ground just outside the booth. "Do you think our mystery girl dropped this?"

Nancy picked it up and studied it closely. The bracelet had braided loops of yarn that tied around the wrist. One of the loops had torn. When she flipped the bracelet over, she noticed the initials RJT embroidered in red yarn.

"Maybe the caller dropped it on purpose," Nancy said as she pocketed the bracelet.

"Or maybe she caught it on something, and it tore," Bess suggested.

"Right," Nancy said. "But whatever happened, this seems to be the area we need to search."

She slowly walked toward the building nearest the booth. It was a two-story warehouse with boarded-up doors and broken windows. Above the main entry was a crooked sign that read Northern Freight. A gravel drive wound past the side of the building and around to the back.

"If the railroad tracks are behind the building, I bet that drive leads to them," Nancy said, pulling a flashlight from her shoulder bag. "George, why don't you get the flashlight from my glove compartment? You and Tony can search the front of the warehouse, then head around to the right. Bess and I will start down the drive. We'll meet around back."

"Roger, boss." George saluted, then went over to the car.

Bess waved goodbye to Tony, then reluctantly followed Nancy down the drive.

"Gee, you could've let *me* go with Tony," she muttered.

Nancy chuckled. "Not if I wanted anything accomplished," she teased her friend. "Besides, what would Kyle think if he heard you were strolling in the dark with a handsome guy?"

Bess sighed. "Probably nothing. He's too busy thinking about law school."

"Hmm," Nancy replied, not really focusing on Bess. She was concentrating on finding evidence.

Glass and gravel crunched under Nancy and Bess's feet as they slowly walked down the drive. Nancy swung her flashlight to the right, illuminating the side of the brick building. Then she swung it to the left. Weeds rustled in the wind along the edge of the drive.

"This is spooky," Bess whispered. She was behind Nancy, clutching at the back of her friend's jacket. At the rear of the building was a parking lot. Nancy counted five loading bays on the back of the warehouse, all of which were shut tight. There was a beat-up old car at the very end of the lot.

She shone her light beyond it toward a grassy field behind the parking lot. When she swept her beam in an arc, the light picked up the glint of steel tracks.

"There they are!" she whispered.

Bess followed Nancy across the lot and into the grass. When they reached the tracks, Nancy's heart began to pound, and the hair prickled on the back of her neck.

She swung her beam to the right. Several railroad cars loomed nearby, empty and dark. Had something happened in one of them?

Then she swung her light to the left. Behind her, Bess let out a muffled scream as the beam of the flashlight shone on a dark mound sprawled on the tracks.

Nancy gasped.

It was a body.

Chapter
Three

O H, NO!" BESS CRIED OUT, covering her mouth with both hands.

For a second Nancy stood frozen on the railroad tracks. She'd been expecting something terrible, but not this! Then she took a deep breath and said quietly, "We'd better check it out." Quickly she walked down the tracks, followed by Bess. The body was facedown, but when she stooped next to it, she could tell it was a guy.

"Is he—" Bess stammered.

One of the guy's arms was flung out to the side. Nancy pressed her fingers against the wrist, searching for a pulse. Finding nothing, she felt for the pulse at the neck.

She shivered. "He's dead. You'd better get Tony and George."

Bess raced back through the weeds, calling

loudly, while Nancy studied the body. She didn't want to disturb anything, but her eyes hunted for clues.

"Bess said you found a body. . . ." Tony's voice trailed off, and George inhaled sharply as the three came up beside Nancy.

"Yeah. He's slightly warm, so he hasn't been dead that long." Nancy stood up. "We'd better call the police."

"I'll go!" Bess and Tony chorused. Turning, they both took off for the pay phone.

"I don't think they wanted to hang around," George said, nervously shifting from foot to foot. "Not that I blame them. Any idea who it is?"

Nancy shook her head. "I can't see his face, and I don't want to disturb him."

"This place is so deserted," George said. "I wonder what he was doing here?"

"I don't know, but maybe the mystery caller does."

"That's right," George said. "I forgot all about her. If she saw this guy get murdered, no wonder she freaked out."

"We don't know yet if he was murdered," Nancy said as she started walking down the tracks. "Look, George." She motioned to her friend. When George jogged up beside her, Nancy pointed to the right. The grass had been flattened in two parallel lines. "It looks like a car drove up to the railroad tracks and stopped."

"Nancy! George!" Nancy heard Bess's anxious call from the other side of the field.

"We'd better go back to the driveway," Nancy said. "The police will be mad if we stomp all over the area."

"We called the cops. They'll be here any minute," Bess said when Nancy and George met her and Tony behind the warehouse.

Ten minutes later a police cruiser and an unmarked car zoomed up the warehouse drive. The unmarked car screeched to a halt a foot away from the teens. When the detective climbed out, Nancy recognized him immediately. It was B.D. Hawkins, the officer who had helped Nancy and Bess recover Bess's stolen Camaro.

"Hey! Nancy and Bess!" B.D.'s roguishly handsome face broke into a big smile. He was wearing the same worn leather jacket and cowboy boots as the first time they had met him. A baseball cap covered his longish hair.

"Hello, B.D." Nancy introduced everybody, then asked the detective if he was back on the homicide squad.

He nodded. "Yup. After you helped us clean up that car theft ring, I was transferred back where I belong. So where's this body?"

Nancy pointed toward the tracks. B.D. waved at the two uniformed patrol officers climbing out of the squad car. "Check it out! Then secure the crime scene," he called. Turning his attention back to the teens, he said, "I trust you four didn't disturb anything."

"Uh. I felt his pulse and neck to make sure he was dead," Nancy said apologetically. "And we walked around a bit, so we left some footprints."

"Of course, if we hadn't been walking around, we wouldn't have found the body," Bess chimed in.

B.D. crossed his arms. "And what were you guys doing hanging around a deserted warehouse late at night?"

"Uh . . ." Nancy stammered, then looked over at Tony. She knew hotline conversations were confidential. How much could she tell the detective?

"That's okay, Nancy," Tony assured her. "Since there's been a murder, we'd better cooperate with the police. The caller may be in over her head."

B.D. raised one eyebrow. "Mind telling me what's going on?"

With Bess and George's help, Nancy told him all about the call to the hotline and how they'd found the body.

Then she took the embroidered bracelet out of her pocket and handed it to B.D. "We found this outside the phone booth over there," Nancy added. "It might belong to the caller."

Just then a female patrol officer approached through the weeds. "The guy's dead all right," she said.

B.D. nodded. "Radio for the lab technicians and the medical examiner, then interview these kids. I want separate statements."

While the teens waited, the police officer went back to her patrol car, and B.D. went back to the unmarked car. He returned a few moments later with a camera with built-in flash.

"May I come with you?" Nancy asked.

B.D. hesitated, then shrugged. "Sure. Carla can take statements from your friends, and we can get your statement later. As I recall, you've got a good eye for evidence, and I could use your help."

Nancy showed the detective where she and Bess had been when they discovered the body. Then they walked down the tracks, careful to stay out of the way of the second officer, who was cordoning off the area with yellow tape.

When they reached the body, B.D. raised his camera and shot a dozen pictures from different angles. Then he crouched down.

"Doesn't look like theft," he said, pointing to the dead guy's back pocket. Nancy could see the rectangular bulge of a wallet.

B.D. slipped on rubber gloves, then gingerly pulled the wallet from the pocket and opened it. "Paul Remer. And he has twenty bucks still on him. Recognize the name?"

"No. But if he's from the area, Tony might."

"Let's get him over here." Standing up, he called out to Tony, then glanced at Nancy. "I'm

23

going to turn the body over. Think you can handle it?"

Nancy nodded. Grabbing one arm, B.D. carefully rolled the body onto its back. Nancy suppressed a gasp. Paul Remer's jacket was unzipped, and his T-shirt was stained with blood.

"Knife wound," B.D. commented. "And look at this." He pointed to the shirtfront where someone had slashed a crude letter *N* in the fabric. *"N* is the sign of the Nighthawks. I'd say this was gang related."

"The Nighthawks!" Tony exclaimed behind Nancy.

B.D. nodded. "Yeah. You know the guy?"

"His name's Paul Remer. He works at the teen center," Tony said, shifting uneasily from one foot to the other. "Look, Detective Hawkins, I grew up in this area and know members of the Nighthawks. They may be into some stupid stuff, but they've never been violent."

"Until now," B.D. said tersely.

More than an hour later, Nancy, Bess, Tony, and George climbed wearily back into the Mustang.

Nancy was turning off Fourteenth Street when Tony sat up in his seat and snapped his fingers. "Wait a minute! I think I might know who our mysterious caller is."

"What?" Nancy took her eyes off the road for a moment to look at Tony. "Who is she?"

"I've seen Paul at the center with a girl," Tony said. "I don't know her name, but she rooms with one of the hotline volunteers, Billie Peters. I think Billie's letting her stay at her apartment until she finds her own place."

"I think we should check it out." Nancy looked in the rearview mirror at Bess and George. "It's late, guys. What do you think?"

"Let's do it," George said, and Bess nodded.

"What about the police?" Tony asked.

Nancy stopped for a red light. "Let's see if we find anything at the apartment. Then I'll call B.D." She faced the windshield again. "Where to?"

Twenty minutes later, Nancy, Bess, and George were following Tony down the third-floor hall of an apartment house not far from the teen center. One dim bulb glowed overhead, spotlighting the graffiti scribbled across the stained wallpaper.

"Nice place," George commented.

"It's cheap," Tony said over his shoulder. He stopped in front of apartment 3A. "This is where Billie lives. You guys met her the other day when you watched the hotline in action."

"I remember," Bess said. "She looks like a tackle for a girls' football team."

"Yeah, that's Billie." Tony raised his fist and

knocked on the door. With a squeal of rusty hinges, it opened several inches.

"That's weird," Tony said. "It's open."

Nancy peered into the darkness inside. After pushing the door all the way open, she cautiously stepped into the apartment. Tony, George, and Bess followed so close behind that Nancy could hear their breathing.

For a second she stood still, waiting for her eyes to get used to the dark. Except for the sound of dripping water from a faucet, the apartment was silent.

"We'd better turn on the light," Bess suggested. "I don't want to trip over a body."

George groped along the wall by the door but couldn't find a light switch.

"Hello! Is anyone home?" Nancy called as she reached for the flashlight in her shoulder bag. Turning it on, she walked gingerly down a short hallway to what looked like a small living room. When she swung the flashlight around the room, she could see the whole place had been ransacked. The cushions and pillows had been tossed off the sofa, pictures ripped off the walls, and the rug kicked into a corner. A floor lamp had been knocked over, and its shade was dented. Two wooden chairs were on their sides.

"What in the world happened here?" Tony asked. He was still standing by the doorway as he surveyed the small room.

"I'd say someone was looking for something,"

Nancy said. "Let's check out the rest of the place."

The four walked through a doorway into a tiny kitchen. Nancy found the switch and flicked on the overhead light. All the drawers had been pulled out and the cupboards emptied. Cans, boxes, and silverware lay scattered across the floor. George opened a door to the left of the refrigerator. It was a tiny bathroom.

"Nothing in here but a big mess," she said. "Someone even searched the medicine cabinet."

"What do you think they were looking for?" Tony asked.

Nancy shook her head. Then she noticed Bess wasn't in the kitchen with them. "Where's Bess?" she asked George.

Suddenly a shrill scream pierced the air.

Chapter

Four

BESS!" NANCY YELLED as she lunged through the doorway into the living room. In the semi-darkness, she could just make out two people sprawled on the floor. One was sitting on top of the other's back.

"Nancy, help!" Bess screeched from flat on the floor.

Nancy swung her flashlight into the face of the person on top of her friend. It was Billie Peters.

"Hey, let her go!" Nancy demanded. She grabbed Billie's arm with her free hand and tried to pull her off. Billie didn't budge. "We're not the people who ransacked your place. We're from the hotline."

Squinting in the beam of the flashlight, Billie stared at Nancy, a confused expression on her face. Still she didn't let go of Bess's right arm, which she had twisted behind Bess's back.

"Billie, it's me, Tony," the hotline coordinator quickly said from behind Nancy. He and George were standing in the kitchen doorway. "It's okay. Let her go."

"Tony?" Billie said. "What are you doing here? I thought I was being robbed."

"Uh, I think you already were," Tony said as Billie climbed off Bess.

Reaching down, Nancy helped her friend to a sitting position. "Are you all right?"

"No." Bess glared angrily at Billie. "She almost tore off my arm."

"I did not," Billie retorted. "You're just in lousy shape."

For a few moments Billie's gaze darted suspiciously from Nancy to Tony. She was wearing a worn corduroy jacket over a blue sweater and jeans. Her thick brown hair was pulled back in a ponytail, and she wasn't wearing any makeup. She had strong features and snapping eyes, and was almost as tall as Tony.

"I want to know what you're doing here," she demanded. "And I want to know now."

Tony exhaled. "Oh, boy." He looked at Nancy. "Maybe you'd better explain."

"How about if I see whether or not the floor lamp works first?" George suggested.

"And I'd better call the police," Nancy added,

heading over to the coffee table, where she'd spotted a phone. "B.D. is going to want to investigate this."

Reaching out one hand, Billie grabbed Nancy's wrist with a grip like steel. "Oh, no, you don't. Not until you explain what's going on."

Nancy locked eyes with Billie but then sighed. "That's fair," she finally said, and slowly, Billie let go of her wrist.

While Tony gave Bess a hand up, George found an outlet and plugged the lamp in. She turned the switch, and light flooded the room. After putting the cushions back on the sofa and picking up the two wooden chairs, everyone sat down except for Billie. Tony took one of the chairs. Bess and George sat down on the couch, and Nancy perched on the arm of the sofa.

Frowning, Billie remained standing in the middle of the room, her arms crossed over her chest as she surveyed the foursome. "Okay, now explain."

Nancy began with the call to the hotline. When she mentioned the murder, Billie's mouth dropped open, and her shoulders stiffened.

"Paul Remer is *dead?*" she repeated.

"Yes. Did you know him?" Nancy asked.

Billie nodded. "From the teen center. And he and Rachel were sort of dating."

"Rachel's your roommate?" Nancy asked. When Billie nodded, she added, "Do you think she was with him tonight? Could she be the hotline caller?"

Billie put up her hands in protest. "Whoa, there. You sound like a cop."

Tony leaned forward. "Nancy's just trying to find out what happened, Billie."

"Well, don't ask me," Billie retorted. "I barely know Rachel, except to tell you that her last name is Thackett. I met her a week or so ago. She came into the teen center with Paul. He was asking around about a place for her to crash.

"She was willing to pitch in for the rent just for sleeping on the sofa, so I figured she could stay here awhile. Besides, I work until one in the morning," she said, pulling a waitress apron from her jacket pocket and holding it up, "and she was gone during the day. So we never even saw each other."

"What did she do all day?" Nancy asked.

Billie shrugged. "How should I know? She met Paul at the community college, but I don't think she was taking courses there."

"Though Paul was taking courses," Tony said.

Bess slumped back on the sofa and yawned. "Now can Nancy call the police? It's getting late."

"I'll say." George glanced down at her watch. "It's almost two o'clock."

"Police!" Billie snorted. "What for? It's not like whoever broke in could've found anything valuable enough to steal."

31

"I think the break-in might be related to the murder," Nancy explained. "Someone could have been searching for something."

Tony looked puzzled. "Like what?"

Nancy stood up and began pacing. "I'm not sure. But what if the murderer knew there was a witness? And what if he or she thought it was Rachel?"

"You mean the murderer was looking for Rachel?" Bess's eyes widened.

"Or since they couldn't find her, they were looking for something to lead them to Rachel." Nancy stopped in front of the phone. "Whatever happened, we need to call the police. May I?"

Reluctantly, Billie nodded her head.

After she'd talked to B.D., Nancy hung up the phone, spun around, and faced Billie. "Any idea where Rachel is now?"

Billie shook her head emphatically. "Usually when I come in after work, she's sound asleep on the sofa." She sighed and pushed a strand of hair off her cheek. "Look, I wish I could help you more, but I barely know her."

"Maybe someone at the teen center knows her better," George suggested.

Tony nodded. "Or Mr. A might have some information that could help us."

"Where did Rachel keep her things?" Nancy asked. "That may give us a clue about where she's gone."

Billie pointed to an open door on the other side of the living room. One glance told Nancy that the intruder had carefully searched the small closet, too.

A suitcase had been emptied onto the floor and all the clothes ripped off the hangers. Nancy glanced quickly at the clothes—they were expensive. Stooping down, Nancy pulled the suitcase closer. It was made of very good leather, and under the handle she noticed that the initials RJT had been embossed in gold.

A gasp from above caused Nancy to tilt her head up. Bess was standing behind her, looking down at the suitcase.

"Those are the same initials that were on the bracelet!" she exclaimed.

"Right. Which is pretty good proof that we've found our hotline caller." Nancy stood up.

There was a loud rap on the door. "Nancy? It's B.D.," a voice called. The detective poked his head into the apartment, then entered, followed by a crime technician and the same two officers who'd been at the railroad tracks.

"Hey. You didn't tell me the entire police department was going to come," Billie accused Nancy.

B.D. flashed his badge. "Miss, I'm sorry for the inconvenience, but if this is related in any way to the murder of Paul Remer, we need to check it out carefully. I'd like you to go through every room with Officer Simpson and see if anything was taken," he said, gesturing to the policewoman now at his side.

"Oh, great," Billie muttered as she slipped off her coat and threw it onto the arm of the sofa. "Just what I want to do at two in the morning." She headed toward a small hallway off the living room. "Did anyone check my room for damage?" she asked.

"No," Nancy said. "We had only gotten to the kitchen when you came in."

"If my room looks half as bad as the rest of this place, I'll be up all night, cleaning," Billie said angrily.

Officer Simpson followed her.

After Billie and the police officer left, B.D. directed the technician to check for any physical evidence and sent the second patrol officer out into the hall to wake up the other tenants and question them.

"How did the intruder break in?" he asked Nancy.

"I didn't even have a chance to check," she answered.

Turning around, B.D. scrutinized the door lock. "Pretty flimsy. You could pick it with a paper clip." He glanced at Bess, George, and Tony, then looked at Nancy, who was standing beside him. "So what're you guys doing here, anyway? Wasn't a murder enough excitement for one night?"

Bess sighed. "It was enough for me."

"Me, too," George agreed.

"It's all my fault," Tony said. "I thought maybe I knew who the hotline caller was." He told B.D. about seeing Paul Remer around the teen center with a girl. Then Bess and George filled in the rest of the story.

B.D. frowned. "So you thought you'd check it out instead of telling me?"

"We'd already left the warehouse when I thought of it," Tony said, then looked at Nancy for help.

"I decided not to bother you unless we found something," Nancy said, crossing her arms over her chest. When the detective remained silent, she said, "Look, B.D. We think we have proof our caller lives here." Nancy waved her hand toward the closet. "The initials on the suitcase match the ones on the bracelet. The girl's name is Rachel Thackett, and my guess is the place was ransacked right after the murder."

"Hmm." B.D.'s frown disappeared as he strode to the closet and checked out the suitcase. Then he turned to face Nancy. "So you think Rachel saw whoever murdered Paul and the killer saw Rachel?"

Nancy nodded. "Which means if the killer knows where she lives, he or she obviously knows *who* she is. That must be why Rachel didn't come back here. And unless she has a good place to hide, I'd say she's in big trouble."

"That's for sure," B.D. agreed. "Especially since the murder looks like the work of the Nighthawks. They know the area well enough that they wouldn't have much trouble tracking her down."

"So you're sure the gang was responsible?" Tony asked the detective.

"Not a hundred percent. But I called the detective who keeps track of the gangs. It seems that Paul Remer was a member of the Nighthawks until about a month ago when he went to the police with some information about Kip DiFranco, the Nighthawks' leader."

Tony frowned, and B.D. went on. "Kip had been linked to a recent break-in at a drugstore in the area. But Kip had had an alibi for the night of the burglary, so he was released. A few days later, Paul came in and told the police he could prove Kip was lying about his alibi. Paul's information led to Kip being arrested again."

"Whew." Nancy gave a low whistle. "Was Kip charged?"

B.D. shook his head. "No. The drugstore clerk didn't pick Kip out of the lineup, so he was set free. But, according to the cops in the area, that doesn't mean DiFranco wasn't guilty. They just didn't have enough proof for a conviction."

Tony shook his head. "I can't believe it. Theft, murder. The Nighthawks used to be basically a bunch of punks who only acted like big shots."

"Revenge can be a powerful motivation for violence," B.D. said solemnly.

"So you think Kip DiFranco killed Paul because Paul turned him in to the police?" Bess asked.

"Yup," B.D. said firmly. "I think if we catch DiFranco, we'll be able to prove that he murdered Paul Remer."

Suddenly there was a loud gasp from the hallway leading to the bedroom. Nancy jerked her head around. Billie Peters was standing frozen in the threshold, a shocked expression on her face.

"Kip couldn't have murdered Paul!" Billie cried out.

Then before anyone could stop her, she grabbed her coat, flung open the door, and raced down the building's hallway!

Chapter

Five

"BILLIE, WAIT!" Nancy cried as she took off after the girl. When she reached the banister in the hall, she peered over the railing. She could see the top of Billie's head about two flights below.

"We've got to catch her," B.D. said beside Nancy. The two plunged down the stairs, but when they reached the first floor, they found the front door wide open—and no Billie.

Side by side, Nancy and B.D. raced outside, coming to a halt on the top step of the stoop. Nancy looked right, then left, only to find the street and sidewalks deserted.

"Where could she have disappeared to so fast?" B.D. asked.

Nancy ran down the outside steps, then headed toward the alley on the left side of the building. "Maybe down here. Or over there." She jerked her thumb toward the shadowy stores and abandoned buildings across the street. "She knows the neighborhood a lot better than we do."

"Man!" B.D. smacked his fist against his palm. "Me and my big mouth. She obviously knows Kip DiFranco. If she gets the word out that we're looking for him, he'll go into hiding, and we'll never pick him up."

Just then Tony, Bess, and George appeared on the stoop.

"I'm calling descriptions of Billie, Rachel, and Kip into the precinct," B.D. told Nancy. "Every patrol car in the area will be looking for them." With long strides, B.D. headed for his unmarked car.

Nancy joined her friends in front of the apartment house. "I must be the only one glad to see Billie go," Bess remarked.

"Why?" Tony asked. "Because she flattened you?"

Bess put her hands on her hips. "No—because she said I was in lousy shape! When does that self-defense class you were talking about start, Tony?"

"Tomorrow."

"Then sign me up," Bess said resolutely. "That's the last time I get tackled!"

"Boy, I hope I can stay awake on the phone today," George said Tuesday morning as she and Nancy headed up the stairs of the teen center. "I don't think a hotline caller would find snoring very helpful."

Nancy laughed. "We didn't get much sleep, did we."

"You can say that again. You dropped me off about three." George opened the door to the hotline office. "And here we are back at the hotline at nine."

Nancy pulled off her jacket, then draped it on the back of a chair. The room was chilly, and only a thin stream of sunlight shone through the windows. The effect was far from cheery.

With a big yawn, George sat down behind one of the desks. She put her head down on the desktop. "Oh, what I wouldn't give for my nice cozy bed."

"You're beginning to sound like Bess," Nancy teased.

"Don't mention her name to me," George grumbled. "It's not fair that she gets to sleep in."

"Well, we did promise Tony we'd take this morning shift," Nancy reminded George. "He says mornings can be really busy, too. This is when dropouts and kids who are too depressed to go to school need someone to talk to. Besides, there's always a chance Rachel may call."

George raised her head and looked at Nancy. "So that's why you're so wide-awake. You're still keyed up from last night."

Nancy nodded. "I keep wondering where Rachel is hiding and thinking about how scared she must be. I'm glad that Tony said he'd ask around the center about her this morning. Maybe he can find out where she and Billie are."

"B.D. might find out something, too," George added.

"Right. He was going to track down Rachel's and Billie's families. Rachel may have headed for the safety of home," Nancy suggested.

"Wherever that is," George said.

Nancy sat down on the edge of the desk. "That's another mystery," she mused. "Rachel's suitcase was top quality, and so were her clothes. I wonder why she ended up hanging around the teen center and sleeping on someone's second-hand sofa."

The shrill jangle of one of the phones startled both the girls. Nancy reached for it. Then the other phone in front of George rang, and she answered it.

"Hello. Help Is Here Hotline. Nancy speaking." The greeting was becoming automatic.

"Nancy?" The voice on the other end was breathless. "Has Kyle called you yet?"

"Bess? Is that you? I figured you'd sleep until noon."

"I would have, only I'm trying to get in touch with Kyle. My parents said he called several times last night wondering where I was."

"Did you call him at work?" Nancy asked.

"Yeah, but he's off with your dad somewhere. By mistake, my parents told him I'd be at the hotline this morning, so Kyle may show up looking for me. Tell him I'll be at the center around noon. We can have lunch together when you guys get off."

"Okay."

George shot Nancy a quizzical look when Nancy hung up. "Who was that?"

"A hysterical caller," Nancy joked. "How about yours? It wasn't Rachel, was it?"

George shook her head. "Don't worry. I'll hand it over to you if it is."

"Hey, you two look gorgeous even without your beauty sleep," Tony greeted the girls as he strode into the room. He was wearing his usual jeans, sweatshirt, and handsome smile.

"Did you find out anything about Rachel or Billie?" Nancy asked eagerly.

Tony jerked his head back. "What? No 'Hi, how are you, Tony?'"

George laughed. "Solving mysteries comes first with Nancy," George explained. "But I'll ask how you are."

"I'm fine, despite the wild time I had last night with you two and Bess." He grinned as he sat down on the chair in front of Nancy's desk. "And, yes, I did find out something."

Nancy opened her mouth to speak, but Tony quickly held up both hands. "Don't get too excited, it wasn't much. Apparently, Paul told Mr. A that he'd met Rachel at the community college. He was handing out teen center pamphlets after one of his classes."

"So Paul was taking courses," George said.

"Right. Rachel hung around asking questions, and Paul offered to bring her to the center. He introduced her to Mr. A. That was about a week and a half ago. Rachel told Mr. A she had no place to stay and hinted that she'd left home kind of abruptly. But Mr. A told me he was pretty certain Rachel was eighteen, so legally she could be on her own."

"Hmmm." Nancy frowned thoughtfully. "Did he say anything about Paul's murder?"

Tony let out his breath. "He was pretty shaken up about it. The police contacted him first thing this morning, since Paul was living at the center."

Nancy looked startled. "Really? You didn't tell me that."

Tony shrugged. "I guess Mr. A told me, but with the hotline, the groups, and school, I didn't pay much attention. Mr. A said he was bunking on the third floor. In exchange for a place to stay, he was doing some of the renovation work— painting, sanding, stuff like that—and helping Mr. A out in the office. Mr. A told me today that he liked having someone here all night in case the center was broken into or vandalized. Plus, Paul was supposedly pretty good with figures."

"It seems that Mr. A put a lot of trust in Paul," George commented.

"Paul was a good guy. Even before he left the Nighthawks, he was working hard to turn his life around. Mr. A thought of him as one of the center's success stories."

"And now he's dead," Nancy said, shaking her head.

Just then Kyle walked into the hotline office. "Hi. Is Bess here yet?" he asked, unbuttoning his overcoat.

Nancy shook her head. "She called and said she'd be in at noon. Why aren't you at work?"

"I had to deliver some papers for your dad." He patted the bulging pocket of his coat, then looked over at Tony. "So, were all of you out last night playing cops and robbers?"

"Until three in the morning," George said with a groan.

"Three?" Kyle raised one brow.

"Three," Tony replied. Leaning back in the chair, he crossed his arms across the University of Illinois emblem on his sweatshirt and met Kyle's gaze.

Nancy rolled her eyes. Kyle was acting jealous, and it almost looked to her as if Tony was egging him on. "Bess will be here at twelve," she told Kyle.

He turned his attention back to Nancy. "Maybe we can all have lunch together."

"Sounds good to me," George said.

"Me, too," Tony said. "The hotline's closed from twelve to three."

Kyle stared at him, then shrugged. "Sure, why not? I'll call Bess and let her know."

With a nod goodbye, he turned and left.

Tony started to chuckle. "I don't think Bess's boyfriend likes me much."

"Hey, Kyle's a great guy," Nancy defended him. "It's just that he knows he's leaving soon for law school, and I don't think he and Bess have really talked about what's going to happen when he goes."

Just then the phone on Nancy's desk rang. She picked it up. "Help Is Here Hotline. Nancy speaking."

"Nancy? Are you the same volunteer I talked to last night?" a voice whispered into the phone. It was the girl who had called the night before! Quickly, Nancy gestured to Tony and George to keep their voices low.

"Yes. It's me. Are you all right?"

"Um. Yes. I—" The caller took a deep breath. "I was wondering if anyone at the teen center knew anything about . . . um . . ."

Nancy decided to level with her. "Paul Remer's death?"

"Yes! I was so afraid to tell you anything last night, but I wanted the police or someone to find him," the caller said, her words tumbling out in a relieved rush.

"The police discovered the body late last night," Nancy explained. "They also discovered

45

a bracelet in a nearby phone booth with the initials RJT. Was it yours?"

There was a long silence. Finally the caller asked, "Are the police there now?"

"No," Nancy said. "This is just between you and me."

"It was my bracelet. I must have snagged it on something when I called the hotline. I was so freaked out, I didn't even notice it was gone."

Nancy paused, then said, "I want you to know that you can trust me."

"What do you mean?" the girl asked.

"I think I know your name. Is it Rachel?"

There was a sharp intake of breath. "How'd you know?"

Nancy told Rachel about Tony's hunch and how they had checked out Billie's apartment. She didn't tell her what Detective Hawkins suspected about the Nighthawks and Kip DiFranco.

"We're worried about you," Nancy added. "You're running away from something, and we'd like to help."

Suddenly Rachel burst into tears. "You're right. I *am* running away. But you can't help. No one can," she sobbed into the phone. "Because I know who murdered Paul Remer!"

Nancy hitched in her breath. "Rachel, if you witnessed the murder, the killer could be after you. Rachel—" Nancy pleaded.

But then she heard a click, followed by the humming of the dial tone.

Chapter

Six

I DON'T BELIEVE IT!" Nancy exclaimed, banging down the receiver. "I lost her again!"

"Did she say where she was?" George asked. She and Tony were watching Nancy closely.

"No. But we were right. She says she knows who murdered Paul." Nancy picked up the phone again. "I'd better call B.D." She dialed and was soon put through to the detective. Nancy told him all about Rachel's call.

"I'm going to get a court order to have the phone company trace all the hotline calls. We should be able to do it by this afternoon," B.D. told Nancy. "That way, if Rachel calls again, at least we'll be able to figure out where she's calling from. We know she hasn't gone back to the apartment because I have an officer keeping an eye on it. Mrs. Thackett was interviewed, but she said she hasn't seen Rachel in almost two weeks. And we still haven't found Billie."

Nancy talked to the detective for a few more minutes while George and Tony listened intently to Nancy's end of the conversation.

"Well?" Tony prompted as soon as Nancy hung up.

"He's worried, too. The police can't find either Billie or Rachel. They did talk to Mrs. Thackett, Rachel's mom. She said that Rachel left home almost two weeks ago after an argument, and she hasn't seen her since. The police are going to ask the phone company to trace all incoming calls to the hotline."

Tony frowned. "Wait a minute. I don't like the sound of that. If our callers find out, they'll quit calling."

"The police are only interested in Rachel's call," Nancy explained. "They won't be listening in to all hotline calls, just getting a report from the phone company that pinpoints where the calls were made from. If Rachel's the key to cracking Paul's murder, the police need to get her in protective custody."

"Well, when you put it like that, it makes sense," Tony said.

"But what's really worrying B.D.," Nancy said, "is that the police can't find Kip DiFranco. It's as if he just vanished. And the other gang members aren't cooperating either."

Tony frowned. "Do the police think Kip's after Rachel?"

"I don't know." Nancy sighed.

Just then both phones rang, and for the next hour, George and Nancy were kept busy with callers. It was almost noon when Bess and Kyle came into the office. Tony had left at ten to run a therapy group.

"Ready for lunch?" Bess asked. Her arm was linked with Kyle's. She was wearing a beret that matched the beige turtleneck sweater she had on under her coat. Nancy could tell she'd spent a lot of time on her hair and makeup.

"I don't know if we're dressed for it," Nancy said, glancing down at her jeans.

Bess waved away her protest. "We're just going to the Riverside. It's casual dress for lunch."

Nancy was telling Bess and Kyle everything that had happened that morning when Tony walked in carrying a clipboard. "Hey, Bess. Did you say something about joining my self-defense class?"

"Yes." Bess's face brightened.

Tony handed her the clipboard. "It starts this evening at seven. I've got three more slots."

"Then sign me up, too," Kyle said quickly. "Otherwise, I'll never see you, Bess," he added.

"Oh, good. It should be fun," Bess said, signing her name to the list. Smiling, she handed the clipboard to Kyle.

"Hey, kids," B.D. said, striding into the office.

His hair was tousled, dark shadows circled his eyes, and he obviously hadn't shaved.

"The tracer will be in place after two o'clock," B.D. told the group. "The phone company will record the numbers of all hotline callers and when they called. On this end, the volunteers will have to note the exact time that Rachel calls again so we can match the time to the number. Then we'll get an address from the phone company computer. Tony, you can be responsible for informing the other volunteers what they need to do."

"Gotcha," Tony said.

"Nancy," B.D. said, motioning for her to follow him into the hall, "can I talk to you for a minute?"

"Sure," Nancy said. Once they were in the hallway, she asked, "What's up?"

"How'd you like to stick around and help me out?" he asked. "The precinct couldn't spare another uniformed cop, and I need to interview as many kids as I can at the teen center, to find out who knew Paul Remer."

Nancy nodded her head vigorously. "I'd love to. Just let me tell the guys I can't join them for lunch."

Twenty minutes later Nancy was standing in the doorway of the teen center's recreation room. For a moment she studied the place. The room took up one side of the building's first floor. In the middle, two boys played pool on a brand-new pool table with a brass plaque that read Donated by Henry Haroldson, Sr.

Beyond the pool table two girls played a video game, and along the right side of the room were a new TV, VCR, two sofas, chairs, and a pay phone. Several teens were watching a soap opera. Above one sofa, Mr. A had hung artwork done by kids from the center. Near the door where Nancy stood was a bulletin board filled with job listings and ads.

On the wall across from Nancy, three ceiling-high windows let the sunlight stream in. The whole effect was bright, cheery, and comfortable. Obviously, Mr. A had worked hard to make the center welcoming.

Nancy introduced herself to the two boys playing pool, while B.D. went over to interview the kids watching TV. They looked about twelve years old, and she wondered why they weren't in school.

"No, man, we didn't know Remer. We just saw him around," the taller of the two said. He was shaking his head and frowning seriously. "The dude was always too busy to talk."

Nancy had written down their names in her notebook. The taller one was called Mike.

Danny, the shorter, younger-looking one frowned, too, trying to look just as tough as his friend. "Remer wasn't like Mr. A. That Mr. A,

51

he's cool. Always stops and asks us how we're doing."

Nancy raised one brow. "Do either of you know any members of the Nighthawks?"

Mike and Danny shot each other a furtive glance.

"Uh, no, man. We don't," Mike spoke for the two of them.

Nancy wasn't sure they were telling the truth, but still she wrote down everything they said. Next, she went over to interview the girls.

"Nope, we didn't know either him or his girlfriend." Carisse, the blond one, shook her head until a slicked-back lock of hair fell over her forehead, partially covering one eye.

"Who was his girlfriend?" Nancy prodded.

"Some red-haired girl," Tanya, the flashier of the two, replied. "Looked kind of snotty." Leaning closer to Nancy, she lowered her voice. "But I do remember one thing; Remer and his girlfriend had a big fight yesterday morning."

"A fight?"

"Yeah," Tanya went on. "She must've been in his room on the third floor. I saw them coming down the stairs. She looked like she'd been crying, and he looked mad."

"Hmmm. Thanks." Nancy mulled over the information as she went out into the hall. B.D. was standing in the doorway, talking to a group of older guys in leather jackets.

"Nighthawks?" she whispered when the group went outside.

B.D. shook his head. "Motorcycle nuts."

The two went back into the rec room, grabbed some crackers and soda from the vending machines, then sat down on the sofa farthest from the TV and compared notes.

When they were finished, B.D. rested his head on the back of the sofa. "Not much to go on."

"Except you have to wonder what Paul and Rachel were arguing about the morning before he was murdered." Suddenly Nancy snapped her fingers. "Wait a minute. Tanya said Rachel came down from Paul's room. Maybe that's where she's hiding!"

"We already searched the place early this morning," B.D. mumbled in a sleepy voice. "No one there."

Nancy stood up. "Then you won't mind if I look for myself, right?"

He opened one eye. "You never give up, do you, Drew?" Groaning, he stood up. "Let me check with Mr. Rosensteel."

Nancy followed him into the hall. A few minutes later, Mr. A was leading the two of them up the flight of steps. Arnold Rosensteel was a short, thin middle-aged man. His glasses were perched on the top of his bald head, and he was wearily rubbing his eyes.

"Paul worked for his room. Plus I used donation money to pay for his classes at the college. And I lent him some money to buy an old car," Mr. A said as they walked up to the third floor. "The deal worked out well for both of us. For years I'd been the only full-time employee at the center, and it was getting too much for me. Paul was a hard worker, and he kept his eye on the place."

When they reached the third floor, Mr. A opened a door, then stood back. "His digs weren't the Taj Mahal, but from what he told me, it was the first place he ever had that he could call his own. He had been living in an abandoned building."

"That sounds right," B.D. said. "Remer's mother said she hadn't seen her son in years."

Nancy stepped through the doorway first. The third-floor room was about the size of the down-stairs rec room. To the right of the doorway, in a corner with finished walls, was a cot, a bedside table, and a reading lamp. An open entryway led to a bathroom. The walls of the rest of the large room had been stripped to the framing and brick. There were stacks of lumber and plasterboard, and sawdust sprinkled the floor.

A quick search told Nancy that B.D. was right. There was no place for someone to hide.

"The bathroom is finished," Mr. A pointed out. "The rest will take longer to complete be-cause, well, funds have sort of dried up."

B.D. walked over to the bedside table and

leafed through several books. "Paul was studying accounting?"

"He decided to take business courses," Mr. A said. "Paul had a good head for numbers."

"So this is going to be the dorm," Nancy said as she walked slowly past the bed.

Mr. A's face broke into a bright smile. "Yes. Too many kids run away from home with no idea where they're going or how rough it is on the streets. I hope the center will soon be a safe stop for them."

With a frown of concentration, Nancy continued to study the room. Just then she spied scrape marks in the sawdust on the floor under the eaves. When she bent down and looked closer, she could just make out a partial footprint.

"B.D., did you stomp all over this place when you searched it?" Nancy asked.

"Not where you are. Why?" B.D. set down the book and walked over to where Nancy was crouching.

"Oh, it's probably nothing, except it seems like an odd place to find a footprint."

Mr. A came up beside B.D. "Not if Paul was working over here."

Nancy ran her gaze up the wall that stopped where the eaves began. One brick sticking out about two feet up caught her eye. There were fresh scratches on the edges, and when she ran her fingers along the front, she realized the brick was loose.

"Hey, B.D.," Nancy said over her shoulder, "hand me a screwdriver or something so I can pry this brick out of the wall."

"What did you find?" he asked. Stooping next to her, he passed her a screwdriver.

"I don't know, but from the scrape marks on this brick, I'd say someone worked pretty hard to get it out of the wall." Nancy dug the end of the screwdriver into the loosest side, then used it like a lever until the brick moved enough so that she could pull it out.

Nancy peered into the hole left behind. An envelope had been pushed into it.

"Well, what do you know," B.D. said. After putting on latex gloves, he reached inside and grabbed the envelope. Mr. A stepped closer, trying to get a better look. Nancy held her breath while B.D. lifted out the envelope and opened the unsealed flap.

His eyes grew wide as he looked inside. Slowly, he reached in with two fingers and withdrew a stack of money. On the top was a hundred-dollar bill.

Quickly, B.D. counted through the stack. "Whew. There are fifty hundred-dollar bills in here." With raised brows, he looked over at Nancy, then up at Mr. A. "And I think when we figure out where this five thousand dollars came from, we may just find our murderer!"

Chapter

Seven

"FIVE THOUSAND DOLLARS!" Nancy repeated, her mind spinning.

Still holding the envelope, B.D. stood up and looked at Mr. Rosensteel. "Do you have any idea where it came from?"

The director shook his head.

After replacing the brick, Nancy stood up. She took one last glance around the room, then followed Mr. Rosensteel and B.D. toward the door. The detective had taken a plastic evidence bag from his jacket pocket. After slipping the envelope inside, he sealed the bag and labeled it.

"I'll get the envelope checked for fingerprints," the detective said. "Paul was arrested once and put on probation, so we have a record of his prints. His might not be the only prints on the

57

envelope, but one way or another, we're going to find out how he got hold of this much money."

Mr. Rosensteel ran his hand over his bald head. "I can't imagine he was doing anything illegal," he said. "He really wanted to make something of himself."

Suddenly the squeak of old wood flooring made Nancy whirl toward the door to the hall. Another squeak told her someone was coming up the steps.

Putting his finger to his lips, B.D. motioned Nancy and Mr. A over to the corner by the bathroom. He dropped the evidence bag on the bed and then flattened himself against the wall by the door.

From her hiding place in the corner, Nancy could hear footsteps moving slowly up the stairs, then across the creaking floorboards of the hallway. Suddenly B.D. twirled from his position against the wall and landed in the doorway face-to-face with a woman.

When she saw him, she raised both hands in the air and screamed shrilly. "Don't hurt me! I'll give you everything I have!"

"Hey, relax." B.D. quickly pulled his police shield from his pocket. "River Heights Homicide Squad. Who are you and what are you doing here?"

Nancy stepped from the corner with Mr. A right behind her. The woman, who appeared to be in her late forties, was wearing a calf-length camel hair coat and carrying an alligator purse that matched her high heels. Leather gloves and a silk scarf completed her outfit. She was attractive, except for the angry expression on her face.

"The police!" The woman dropped her hands. "Do you mean to say my taxes pay for this kind of rude treatment?"

"Lady," B.D. said in a stern voice, "please tell me who you are and what you are doing here."

"My name is Helen Tremain Thackett, and I am looking for my daughter, Rachel."

Mr. Rosensteel hurried forward, his hand extended. "I'm so sorry Detective Hawkins frightened you, Mrs. Thackett," he apologized, his face bright red. "We weren't expecting anyone up here."

"B.D.," Nancy whispered, coming to the detective's side. "I thought you interviewed Rachel's mom."

"Two other cops did," he whispered back. Then he turned his attention to the older woman. "I apologize, too, but as you know there's been a murder, so we're being extra cautious. As Mr. Rosensteel said, we weren't expecting anyone up here."

"Hmmph." Mrs. Thackett slid off her gloves and put them into her purse. "I looked for whoever is in charge downstairs, but there was only a mob of teenagers in dirty clothes who directed me up here. I figured if the police couldn't find Rachel, then *I* had better do it."

This time it was B.D.'s turn to bristle. "We're doing everything we possibly can."

"That's true, Mrs. Thackett." Holding out her hand, Nancy introduced herself, then added, "I'm the hotline volunteer who talked to Rachel."

Mrs. Thackett's eyes suddenly filled with tears, and she clasped Nancy's hand in her own. "Oh, if only she hadn't left home. If only she hadn't come—*here.*" She shuddered as she looked around the room.

Abruptly, she dropped Nancy's hand, and her eyes snapped angrily. "This is where that Paul stayed, isn't it?" she asked Mr. Rosensteel.

He nodded. "Yes. He was—"

Stepping forward, she shook her finger in the director's face. "I told Rachel that guy was no good," she interrupted. "I told her if she lived down here, something terrible would happen. If people like you wouldn't encourage kids to stay away from their homes, none of this would happen!"

Mr. A's face reddened with anger. "Your daughter never lived here, Mrs. Thackett. Paul did."

"Mrs. Thackett," B.D. said in a calm voice before the woman could respond to Mr. A. The woman turned her icy gaze to the detective. "I thought you told the officers that you hadn't seen

60

or talked to your daughter since she left. If that's true, then when did you warn her about Paul?"

Good question, Nancy thought. And from the flush creeping up Mrs. Thackett's face, Nancy knew the woman realized she'd made a big mistake.

"Uh, um," Mrs. Thackett stammered. She reached into her purse, pulled out a tissue, and dabbed at her cheeks and forehead. "I did talk to her once on the phone. I guess I forgot to tell the officers."

B.D. raised one brow. "Perhaps you'd better accompany me outside. I'd be interested to hear if there's anything else you forgot to mention." Reaching down, he picked the evidence bag off the bed. A couple of bills that had slipped from the envelope inside showed through the plastic.

Nancy saw Mrs. Thackett's gaze dart to it. A glimmer of alarm showed in the woman's eyes, then just as quickly disappeared.

"So are you any closer to capturing the murderer?" Mrs. Thackett asked B.D. as he escorted her from the room.

"Before you go, Mrs. Thackett," Nancy said quickly, "do you have a picture of Rachel? I'd like to have one to show around."

Again, tears filled the older woman's eyes. "Of course." She reached in her handbag for her wallet, then gave Nancy what looked like a photo from a high school yearbook. "She graduated last spring. Straight A student, chorus, band, debate team, voted Most Likely to Succeed. And here she is nine months later, hiding out like a criminal!"

B.D. murmured soothingly, then put his hand under Mrs. Thackett's elbow and escorted her from the room. When the two left, Mr. A made a disgusted noise in his throat.

"With a mother like that, no wonder Rachel ran away," he said. "She's a cross between a strutting peacock and a man-eating barracuda."

Nancy laughed at the director's description. Then she looked down at the photo. Rachel had thick, wavy red hair, laughing green eyes, and a cheerleader smile. "This should help us find her," she said. "Maybe we can get some copies made and pass them around."

"Good idea." The director sighed. "Things are complicated enough at the center without a murder and a disappearance. I still have a group of teens downstairs waiting to learn how to write résumés and go on job interviews."

As Nancy followed him out the door, his shoulders slumped. "And I'll teach them how to make a good impression, only you know what?"

He stopped on the top step and looked at Nancy. "There aren't any jobs out there for high school dropouts with no skills. I tell the kids to stay in school, but do they listen?" Anger flared in his eyes. "No."

Nancy nodded sympathetically. She knew the director must be under a lot of stress. Even though the center had a board of directors, he was solely responsible for running it.

"Let me know if there's anything I can do," she offered as they went down to the second floor.

Turning, he patted her hand. "Keep looking for Rachel. That will help."

"Okay." Nancy paused outside the door of the hotline office while he continued down the steps to the first floor. For a second, she leaned over the banister. She watched him walk down the steps and disappear. A moment later she caught a glimpse of someone walking in the direction of the front door. Nancy recognized the thick brown hair pulled back in a ponytail.

It was Billie Peters.

Nancy took a deep breath. She had lots of questions to ask Billie, and this time she wasn't going to lose her.

Nancy raced down the stairs. Billie was standing at the open front door, looking at something. She didn't see Nancy come up to her.

"Billie," Nancy said in a firm voice. Taking hold of the girl's lower arm, she pulled her away from the door.

Billie's eyes widened when she saw who it was. "Take your hands off me!" she demanded, chopping at Nancy's fingers. But Nancy was ready. With a quick twist, she yanked Billie's arm behind her back.

"Look, I don't want to hurt you, but I also don't want you running away before you answer some questions," Nancy said quietly. "It's important that we find Rachel. Her life may be in danger!"

Billie stopped struggling.

"Hey, Peters, you okay?" Two teenage boys had come from the rec room and were watching Billie and Nancy with narrowed eyes.

Billie nodded. "I'm all right. Thanks anyway, guys. I'll be ready to start that pool game in a second."

Reluctantly, the two shuffled back into the rec room.

Billie must have come into the center, Nancy thought, while she was on the third floor. She let go of Billie's arm.

"Will you talk to me?" she asked again.

Billie nodded. Rubbing her wrist, she looked at Nancy with new respect. "You've got some pretty good moves."

Nancy laughed, then grew serious. "The police think that Rachel witnessed the murder. We're afraid the killer may be after her. Do you have any idea where she might be hiding?"

Billie shook her head. "No. If I did, I'd tell you, 'cause then Rachel could tell the cops that Kip DiFranco had nothing to do with Paul's murder."

"How do you know he wasn't involved?" Nancy asked.

"I just do. And that's all I'm going to say. There's no way I'm going to tell you or anyone else where Kip is. The cops can lock me up for all I care!"

"Look, Billie, if Kip is innocent, it would be best if he talked to the police."

Throwing back her head, Billie laughed hysterically. "Oh, that's a good one. Ever since Kip skated from that burglary rap, the cops have been dying to find something to pin on him." Her expression hardened. "And they'd just love to get him for murder. Only I know he didn't do it."

She pushed Nancy toward the open doorway and pointed. B.D. was standing beside a blue sedan, talking to Mrs. Thackett. As they watched, B.D. opened the car door for the woman. "That lady is the one the police should arrest," Billie said in a low voice. "Mrs. High Society La-de-da Thackett murdered Paul Remer!"

Chapter

Eight

"RACHEL'S MOM KILLED PAUL?" Nancy asked in an incredulous voice.

"Yup." Billie replied.

In silence the two stood in the doorway of the center and watched Mrs. Thackett's sedan pull away from the curb with B.D.'s car following it. Then Nancy turned and looked at Billie.

"How do you know?"

"Because Sunday night, the day before Paul was murdered, I overheard her tell Rachel that if she ever saw Rachel and Paul together, she'd kill him."

Nancy sucked in her breath. Billie nodded knowingly. "They were in the living room of the apartment."

"Wait a minute. Mrs. Thackett *knew* Rachel was staying with you?"

"Uh-huh," Billie replied, a sarcastic smile curling her lips. "I bet she told you and the cops she'd never seen Rachel since her precious daughter left home."

"You got it." Nancy ran her fingers through her hair. Her mind was going a mile a minute. If Billie was telling the truth, Mrs. Thackett had lied to the police—but why?

Nancy looked over at Billie. "Why don't I buy you a soda, and you can tell me the whole story?"

"I don't know. I promised I'd play pool with those guys you saw. Besides"—Billie began frowning suspiciously—"do you believe me or are you playing cop—you know, acting real nice just so you can get information out of me?"

"I'm definitely not playing cop, Billie, but right now I'm pretty confused," Nancy said. "You just told me some heavy stuff."

"True." Billie started toward the rec room. "Okay. I'll tell you what I know."

Nancy followed, stopping at the machine to buy two sodas. Then she went over to where Billie was sitting on one of the sofas, nonchalantly leafing through a magazine. The two teenage boys had started playing pool. A few girls were clustered around the TV.

Nancy handed Billie a soda, then sat down next to her. "So when exactly did Mrs. Thackett come to the apartment?" she asked as she pulled the tab on her can.

"It was a little after four in the afternoon. I

remember because I was about to leave for my shift at the restaurant. I was changing in the bedroom, so they didn't know I was listening."

"How did she find out where Rachel was?"

Billie shrugged, then took a swig of soda. "I don't know, but that woman wanted Rachel to come home so badly, I think she would've tracked her to the moon. I mean, first she started out nice. You know, 'Please come home, dear. I'm so lonely without you.' But when Rachel said she wanted to be on her own for a while, well, old mom turned ugly real quick. 'You'd better come home or I'll never speak to you again, and you won't get a cent of my money! You'll have to live in a dump like this for the rest of your life!'"

Billie snorted. "That witch. Can you imagine calling my place a dump?"

Nancy started to nod, then quickly shook her head. "So what did Rachel do?"

"She stood up to Mrs. Thackett. She told her that she liked the 'dump' because at least there she was free to make her own decisions. Said she was sick and tired of having her mom run her life. Well, you can imagine how Mrs. Thackett liked that." Billie chuckled. "I could practically feel the anger explode through the walls."

"I can imagine." Nancy remembered how Mrs. Thackett had yelled at both B.D. and Mr. A. "It sounds like she really hated Paul."

"That's for sure. She said everything was his fault—even though Rachel had only met him recently. He had nothing to do with her moving out. She had already left home when she met him, and he was just trying to help her. Anyway, I guess Mrs. Thackett thought Rachel would have moved back home if she hadn't met Paul. So she told Rachel if she saw them together again, she'd kill him."

"Hmmm." Nancy sat back and, slowly sipping her soda, thought about all that Billie had told her. It sounded like the truth. Mrs. Thackett and Rachel probably did have an argument. But what if Billy was exaggerating to throw suspicion off Kip?

There was obviously something going on between Billie and Kip. But Billie had been adamant about not saying anything more about the gang leader, and Nancy didn't want to lose her trust by asking.

"I can see you don't believe me," Billy said, breaking into Nancy's thoughts.

"Hmmm?" Nancy swung her head around. "Oh, no. I'm just trying to fit the pieces together. Somehow I can't imagine Mrs. Thackett stabbing Paul. And how would she have known about the *N* for the Nighthawks?"

Billie frowned. "Good point." For a second, she was silent. Then she took a deep breath and turned toward Nancy. "Look, Drew. The reason why I know Kip DiFranco didn't kill Paul is because I was with him all night."

Nancy must have looked startled because Billie

quickly added, "I worked the afternoon shift on Monday, then spent the evening with Kip at his apartment."

"Why didn't you tell the police?"

Her face flushed. "Because they wouldn't believe me or Kip, that's why." She jumped up. "You don't know what the cops can be like."

Nancy straightened. "But B.D. is different."

"Ha! I'll just bet he is." Bending down, she looked Nancy in the eye. "And don't you go running to him, either." Spinning on her heels, Billie stomped over to the pool table and grabbed a pool cue.

"Will you let me know if you hear from Rachel?" Nancy called to her.

Ignoring her, Billie bent over the table. "Red ball in the corner pocket," she said, setting up her shot.

Nancy stood up, realizing that this was Billie's way of ending the conversation. Slowly, Nancy sauntered into the hall, wondering what she should do with her new information. Since she wasn't sure Billie was telling the truth, she hated to tell B.D. Still, she felt a responsibility to let him know.

Just then George and Tony walked into the center.

"Hey, Nan," George greeted her. "You look like you've had a tough afternoon. You should have had lunch with us at the Riverside."

"Really," Tony said. "We all had the buffet—shrimp, crab legs, oysters, fried clams."

"Gee, thanks for telling me," Nancy said. "I had cheese and crackers out of the vending machine."

Tony and George laughed. Then Tony put one arm around Nancy's shoulders and gave her a squeeze. "We didn't even tell you the best part. Kyle paid for it—to celebrate his acceptance to law school. The guy's not so bad after all."

"How is Bess taking it?" Nancy asked.

George shook her head. "Not very well. To make things worse, Kyle may leave this week. He's had a job offer from a California law firm. Your dad recommended him, and from the way Kyle talked, I'd say he wants to take it. He'd be doing the same kind of work that he does for your dad, but it would be for a big, prestigious firm."

"Kyle is ambitious," Nancy said.

"Right. Plus the company's even offering to pay some of his tuition. Anyway, your dad gave Kyle the afternoon off, so I think he and Bess are finally going to sit down and talk about what's going to happen when he leaves."

"My hunch is Bess will be okay," Tony said, starting up the stairs. "Well, I've got a group this afternoon, and I've got to check that my afternoon-shift volunteers will be here. Nancy, you'll have to fill me in later on what's going on with the case."

"One question before you go. Do you know where Billie works?"

Tony thought for a second. "Yeah, she's a waitress at Ernie's Grill on Main and Thirteenth. Why?"

"I'll let you know later." Nancy waved, then started for the pay phone in the rec room. "And I'll fill you in, too, George, but first I need to call B.D. He should be at the police station by now, and I think he might find my latest news very interesting."

When she finally reached the detective, she told him all about Billie's accusation. By the time Nancy had hung up, George's mouth was hanging open. She'd listened to every word.

"You mean Rachel's mom might be a suspect?"

"I'll tell you in the car," Nancy said. Several kids had come into the center, and Nancy didn't want to broadcast the news.

When they got outside, Nancy headed straight for the Mustang.

"Why do I get the feeling we're going to track down a lead?" George asked, jogging to keep up with her friend.

"Because we are." When they got in the car, Nancy told George about finding the money, Mrs. Thackett's coming to the center, and her conversation with Billie.

George settled her long, athletic frame into the passenger seat. "Wow. What did B.D. think?"

"He was talking to Mrs. Thackett when I called. She claims she was at a benefit for the community theater on Monday night when Paul was killed. He's going to have a man check it out. And he said he'd ask her about the fight she and Rachel had had at Billie's apartment. But from the tone of his voice, I can tell he's still convinced the Nighthawks are the culprits."

After starting the car, she pulled out onto Main Street. "Several store owners on Fourteenth and Main Street can place Kip in the area before the shops closed. In fact, one witness says she saw Kip and Paul together—and they were arguing."

George grimaced. "Ooh. That doesn't sound good. But what did B.D. say when you told him Billie said she was with Kip all night?"

"B.D. figures she's trying to cover for him. And he may be right. When Billie caught us in the apartment, she told us that she'd just gotten off work."

George nodded. "That's right. So you think she just changed her story to help Kip?"

"Maybe. But there's one way to find out." Nancy headed down Main Street. "Since Billie's hanging out at the center, I think it'll be safe to do a little detecting."

Fifteen minutes later Nancy and George were seated at a table at Ernie's Grill. The place was clean and neat with red-and-white checkered tablecloths. Since it was midafternoon, there weren't any other diners. But from the back room, Nancy heard laughter and the sounds of people playing pool.

"I just ate like a horse at the Riverside, but Ernie's meatball sub sounds pretty good," George said as she scanned the plastic-coated menu.

"What can I get you ladies?" the waitress asked when she came up to the table. She was in her fifties. Her graying hair was pulled into a bun and she wore a checkered apron that matched the tablecloth.

"I'm Lil," she said. "And don't order the chili unless you like your food red-hot."

"I'll have iced tea and the Ernie Burger," Nancy said, putting down her menu.

"And I'll take the meatball sub." George grinned. "With mozzarella and green peppers."

When Lil left, George leaned closer to Nancy. "So what do we do now? Ask Ernie if Billie worked here Monday night?"

Nancy looked around. "I don't even know if there is an Ernie."

"Sure there is. He's in the back adding gallons of hot sauce to the chili."

Nancy started to laugh but then put a finger to her lips. "Here comes Lil. Let me do the talking." She waited until the waitress had set the drinks on the table, then said, "My friend and I were in here Monday night, late—between ten and midnight—and I left my jacket in the booth."

"Uh-huh," Lil said in a bored voice.

"I thought maybe our waitress might have picked it up. I think her name was Billie."

Lil tapped her lips with her pencil, stuck out one hip, and thought a second. "Yeah. Billie was working late last night. But she didn't say anything about picking up a jacket. Sorry."

"Did you hear that?" George whispered when Lil left. "Billie *was* working the night Paul was murdered."

"Right." Nancy nodded excitedly. "And if she's lying to protect Kip, that means he must have something to hide—like the murder of Paul Remer!"

Chapter

Nine

Maybe Billie lied about the argument between Rachel and Mrs. Thackett, too," Nancy said to George.

"Wow. Maybe Billie will do anything to protect Kip," George replied.

Just then Lil brought their orders. Nancy's stomach began to growl when she saw the juicy Ernie Burger. She hadn't realized how hungry she was.

When Lil left, George asked, "What are we going to do now?"

"As soon as we finish eating, we need to head back to the center to talk to Billie," Nancy said as she picked up her burger. "She's got some explaining to do!"

* * *

An hour later George and Nancy were standing in the doorway to the rec room. Kids were playing cards and video games. Billie was talking on the pay phone, a serious expression on her face. Her cheeks paled when she saw the two girls, and she hung up quickly.

"I wonder who she was talking to," George said in a low voice.

"Kip, I bet," Nancy whispered back, then strode over to the phone. Before Billie could get past her, Nancy grabbed her arm.

"Hey, Billie, George and I just had a nice meal at Ernie's," she said in a casual tone.

Billie grunted and looked away from her.

"Yeah. And we met a friend of yours named Lil," George added.

Billie looked sideways at the two of them. "And I bet you asked Lil if I worked Monday night."

Nancy raised one brow. "How'd you guess?"

Sighing, Billie pulled her arm from Nancy's grasp. "That was Kip I was talking to. He was really mad at me. He said it would only hurt him if I didn't tell you the truth."

"And what *is* the truth?" Nancy asked.

Billie motioned for Nancy and George to follow her into the hallway. Compared to the rec room, it was fairly quiet. "The truth is Kip had nothing to do with Paul's murder, only he has no alibi." Billie swung around to face Nancy. "And without an alibi, he's dead meat."

"Hmmm." Crossing her arms, Nancy stared at Billie. The girl met her gaze without flinching. *She is* telling the truth, Nancy decided, or at least she thinks she is.

"How about if I meet with Kip and let him tell me the whole story?" Nancy asked. "Then I can go to the police. Maybe they'll believe me."

"You'd have to meet him alone," Billie said.

"No way, Nancy," George said quickly. "That's too dangerous."

"Not if it will clear Kip," Nancy told her friend. "If he *is* innocent, the police need to be searching for the real killer."

"I'll call and arrange it," Billie said. "But it will have to be on our terms."

"I understand."

"Nancy," George said, pulling her friend aside when Billie went back into the rec room. "You can't do this alone."

"I don't have any choice," Nancy replied. "If you were Kip, would you trust anyone?"

"No, I guess not. Still—"

"It's done." Billie marched back into the hallway a few minutes later. "Ten o'clock tonight. Drive to the warehouse where Paul was killed. Park in front, then walk to the tracks. If you're alone and we don't smell any cops, we'll find you."

Nancy nodded. Billie eyed her warily for a second.

"I hope we can trust you, Nancy," she said in a low voice, then strode to the front door, flung it open, and left.

"Whew," George gasped. "You're at least going to let me wait in the car, right?"

Nancy shook her head. "I can't, George. If Kip senses that I haven't followed their directions, he may never come out of hiding. And then this case could really stall, especially since it doesn't look like the police are any closer to finding Rachel."

"Yeah. I guess you're right," George said, but she was still frowning.

"Look, nothing's going to happen," Nancy assured her friend. "But if I don't call you by eleven o'clock tonight, you have my permission to contact B.D. and tell him everything."

"Hey, guys, what's up?" a voice asked behind them.

Nancy and George spun around to see Bess and Kyle entering the teen center. Bess's eyes were red and puffy. Kyle had a sheepish expression on his face.

"We thought we might find you here," Bess said. Reaching out, George gave Bess a hug. "Are you all right?"

Bess looked over at Kyle, then back at her cousin. "Yeah. Kyle and I talked about his leaving and, well, I'm pretty upset, but I think we've worked it out. So where have you guys been?"

Nancy smiled. "That's a long story. Are you here for your self-defense class?"

Kyle nodded. "We thought we'd see if you two wanted some dinner first."

"We just ate," George said. "But we'll keep you company."

Nancy winked at George. "We know the perfect place—Ernie's Grill. And, Kyle, they have your favorite dish just the way you like it—red-hot chili!"

At ten o'clock sharp, Nancy pulled the Mustang up to the warehouse and parked. She turned off the car lights but hesitated before getting out.

Maybe this wasn't such a good idea, she thought. She was alone at a deserted warehouse where someone had been killed. What if Kip *was* guilty? What if he figured Nancy knew too much and needed to be eliminated?

Nancy shook her head, trying to drive away her thoughts. Kip wouldn't be stupid enough to do anything to her, too. That would be too risky.

Besides, this meeting was important. When she'd called B.D. after dinner, he told her they'd found Paul's prints on the envelope, as well as some other prints they couldn't identify, so they had no idea where the money had come from. Also, one of the officers had checked Mrs. Thackett's alibi for Monday night. The ticket taker and two other patrons remembered seeing her arrive at the theater just before eight o'clock.

Taking a deep breath, Nancy opened the car door and swung her legs out. So if Mrs. Thackett had an alibi, that meant Nancy had to figure out if Kip was innocent or just a clever con artist.

Nancy walked slowly down the long drive. Except for the crunching of gravel under her feet, the night was silent.

Where was Kip hiding? she wondered. She remembered B.D. telling her that the gang sometimes met in the old railroad cars.

When she reached the tracks, Nancy stopped and looked around. The moon peeped from behind billowing clouds. She shivered as the wind raced down the tracks. The old railroad cars loomed dark and empty to the right of her. Still, Nancy felt as if eyes were watching her from every shadow.

One cautious step at a time, Nancy made her way down the tracks toward the cars. A noise made her freeze midstep. It was only a soft thud, but Nancy could tell it came from the boxcar nearest her.

"Billie? Are you there?" Nancy called. When there was no answer, she huddled into her down jacket, trying to stop her shoulders from shaking as she walked toward the boxcar.

Nancy peered around the side of the car, but it was so dark she couldn't see anything. She opened her shoulder bag and pulled out her flashlight. But before she could flick it on, a hand clamped down over her mouth and another one grabbed her wrist.

The flashlight clattered to the tracks as Nancy's arm was twisted behind her back and she was pulled roughly backward against someone's chest.

Chapter

Ten

WITH HER FREE ARM, Nancy struck out behind her, but the grip on her wrist tightened painfully, and the fingers over her mouth squeezed her cheeks.

"If you know what's good for you," a voice behind her whispered, "you'll come quietly. All right?"

Nancy nodded and dropped her arm. Without letting go of her, the person pushed her forward. She was guided past the boxcar and up to the ladder of an old caboose.

"Hey! Joey! I need some help here," the voice called, and Nancy knew who her captor was— Billie!

A tall, gangly kid stepped onto the outside platform of the caboose. He grabbed Nancy by the arm and hauled her up the rungs of the ladder.

"Sorry about the rough treatment," Billie said as she swung up next to Nancy. "But we had to make sure you came by yourself. Kip's inside." Billie motioned toward the door of the caboose.

Arms folded, Joey stood to one side. Nancy poked her head into the caboose. Faint streaks of moonlight filtered through the conductor's lookout, and she saw half a dozen faces staring at her.

A lighter flicked on, and a tall guy with hooded gray eyes stepped from the shadows. Thrusting the flame in Nancy's face, he studied her carefully.

"So you're the P.I.," he commented.

Nancy shielded her eyes from the dancing light. "Yes. Nancy Drew. And you're—"

"Kip DiFranco." He flicked the lighter off and held out his hand.

"And this is my gang." Kip waved Nancy farther inside. From what she could make out in the moonlight, everybody was wearing a black leather jacket with the letter *N* studded onto the front.

"So, you're working with the cops," Kip said. "I've read about you in the newspaper. You've solved some pretty wild crimes."

"Some." Nancy stood very straight, hoping her voice sounded strong.

Everyone glared suspiciously at her except for

Kip, who eyed her coolly, his hands shoved in the pockets of his jeans.

"So, Ms. Private Investigator, how can we help each other?" he asked.

"I want to catch the person who murdered Paul Remer."

Kip nodded. "Me, too. Not that I'm all choked up because he's dead," he added, "I just don't like being accused of something I didn't do."

"And what proof is there that you're innocent?"

"I don't have any. That's my problem. I crashed early last night. And I was alone in my apartment. And since I supposedly have a motive for the killing, the cops are going to pin this on me no matter what."

"What do you mean, a motive?" Nancy asked.

Kip's eyes hardened. "Search her," he told Billie, without answering Nancy's question.

Billie ran expert hands down Nancy's sides and back. "She's clean."

"Good." Kip nodded. "If we'd found a wire on you, you would've been in trouble. But since you're clean, I'll tell you the truth. I would have loved to see Paul Remer run out of town. He almost landed me in jail on a burglary charge."

Nancy frowned.

As if in answer to her unasked question, he said, "Yeah. I pulled the job, and because of Remer, the cops caught me. I had an alibi all set up. Friends of mine swore to the police that I was playing pool all night at Ernie's. Only Paul decided to rat on me. He told the cops I wasn't playing pool and that he saw me outside the drugstore minutes before it was robbed."

"Was Paul telling the truth?"

"Uh-huh. Luckily, I got off because the clerk at the store couldn't identify me in the lineup and my friends stuck to their story." He laughed. "Plus, all we got was some change and aspirin. Big heist, huh. Last I heard, the store dropped the charges."

"What about the fact that several store owners saw you arguing with Paul on Monday night not far from the murder scene?"

Kip raised one brow. "Okay, so Remer and I argued. I told him if I saw his ugly face around Nighthawk territory again, I'd kick him out myself." He leaned close to Nancy. "But I didn't say I'd kill him."

"That's right," Joey confirmed. "I was there."

"What did Paul do when you threatened him?" Nancy asked.

"He told me he had more important things to do than argue with a punk like me."

Nancy frowned. "Do you have any idea what he meant?"

Joey, Billie, and Kip shook their heads.

"Any idea who killed him?"

Kip's face brightened. He beckoned to someone hunkered down in the back of the caboose. "Skins, get up here and tell the P.I. what you saw."

A little guy about fourteen pushed his way past the other gang members. His leather jacket hung loose on his skinny frame, his head was shaved bald, and his eyes darted nervously from Kip to Nancy.

"Well, I—I—" he stuttered. Skins flashed Nancy a shy grin, swallowed, then tried again.

"Monday night I—I slept here in the caboose," he said, staring at his feet. "Whenever my dad and I have a big fight, I come here. I sleep on the seat there, and it ain't so bad."

Nancy looked where he was pointing. Under a window that faced the warehouse, there was a long wooden bench. Stepping closer, Nancy peered out the glass. In the moonlight she could see the loading docks, the overgrown field, and a short stretch of the tracks.

"So you were here when Paul was murdered?" she asked, excitement creeping into her voice.

He nodded. "But I didn't see what happened. I woke up when car lights flashed in the window. It took me a second to remember where I was. When I finally sat up and looked out the window, I saw a car in the field behind the warehouse."

Skins glanced hesitantly up at Kip. The leader gave him the thumbs-up sign. After taking a deep breath, the boy finished his story.

"The car lights shone right on the body. I heard the door slam, then the car squealed out of here like it was going to a fire."

Nancy let out her breath. "Did you see the driver?"

"Naw." Skins looked apologetic, but then he gave her a huge grin. "But I know what kind of car it was! A silver Mercedes."

"Thanks, Skins," she said sincerely. Then she reached into her back pocket and pulled out Rachel's picture. "Now, I'd like you all to look at this picture of Paul's girlfriend, Rachel. Maybe someone has seen her in the neighborhood. She witnessed the murder, so if we find her, we can clear up this mystery."

Kip flicked his lighter on so that the gang members could get a good look at the photograph. Nancy watched closely as they passed the picture around and looked at it.

"Nope. We haven't seen her around." Kip was the last person to hand the picture back to Nancy. He flicked off the lighter.

"If you do see her, please call the River Heights Police Department and ask for B. D. Hawkins," Nancy said to the silent, staring faces. "You don't have to give your name."

Several heads nodded.

"And thank you," she added.

"Thank *you*." Kip made a half bow. "For believing us."

But when Nancy finally reached the safety of

the Mustang, she wasn't sure who or what to believe. She just knew she desperately wanted to go home. After calling George to say she was safe, she planned on going straight to bed.

"So let me see if I've got this right," Bess said to Nancy the next morning. She was riding in the front seat of the Mustang, and George was in the back. The three girls were on their way to see B.D. at the police station.

"Mrs. Thackett could be the murderer, only she has an alibi," Bess repeated what Nancy had told them earlier. "Or Kip could be the murderer, although he told you he wasn't. Only he has no alibi."

Nancy laughed. "Right. Simple, huh."

Bess sighed. "Yeah. About as simple as my relationship with Kyle."

Nancy looked at her friend. Bess's mouth was turned down at the corners. "Sorry, Bess. I've been so wrapped up in this case, I'd forgotten about you and Kyle."

"Me, too," George said apologetically. "So what did you two talk about yesterday?"

"I suggested that when he leaves, we date other people." Bess's voice was resigned. "I think it's the only way. We're going to still try to see each other—you know, on holidays and stuff."

George patted her cousin's arm. "Hey, that sounds like a good solution. How did Kyle take the part about dating other people?"

Bess shrugged. "He's not wild about it."

Nancy pulled up in front of the police station, hoping that the case would distract her friend from her troubles for a while. "Let's see if B.D.'s found out anything new."

They found B.D. in his office. There was just one extra chair in his office, and he carried in two others so that all three girls could sit down. Then he sat down behind his desk. The first thing he did when he heard about Nancy's late-night escapade was to groan. "I can't believe you let that punk DiFranco get away, Nancy," he said angrily. "You know we've been looking for him. Maybe I ought to have you arrested for aiding a criminal."

"If I'd let you in on it, Kip would have known," Nancy shot right back. "He's no fool. Then he wouldn't have told me anything."

B.D. muttered something, then swung around in his swivel chair. He stood up and strode to a coffee maker. "You girls want any coffee?" he asked gruffly. Nancy could tell by his unshaven face and the dark circles under his eyes that he probably hadn't made it home the night before.

When they shook their heads, he poured himself a cup, then turned to Nancy. "So you really think this Skins kid was telling the truth about the Mercedes?"

Nancy shrugged. "I think so. Now we just have to figure out who can afford a Mercedes."

"Probably Mrs. Thackett," Bess stated.

Nancy, George, and B.D. turned to her.

"Don't you remember Billie saying Mrs. Thackett told Rachel she wouldn't get any of 'her money'?" Bess reminded them. "And remember Rachel's leather suitcase? And her clothes?"

"Bess is right," Nancy said. "Only when Mrs. Thackett came to the center, she was driving a blue sedan."

"Maybe she has a second car that she's hiding because she thinks it could have been spotted at the scene of the crime," George suggested.

B.D. stopped in the middle of sipping his coffee and glanced suspiciously from Bess to George to Nancy. "Why do I get the feeling you three are cooking up something?"

"Because we are!" Bess exclaimed.

"Look, B.D., I've got an idea," Nancy said excitedly. "You don't have enough evidence to go snooping through Mrs. Thackett's garage, but if we just happened to—"

Holding up one hand to silence her, B.D. strode back to his desk. "I don't want to hear about your plan. In fact, I'm going to pretend you girls weren't even here. But—" Pausing, he looked at them with lowered brows, then suddenly winked and smiled. "If you should happen to spot a silver Mercedes in her garage, I want to be the first to know."

Fifteen minutes later Nancy pulled the Mustang up the circular drive of the Thackett home. It was located in one of River Heights's most expensive neighborhoods. The two-car garage was off to the right of the house. Both doors were shut, and there were no window panels in them.

"Now, remember," Nancy told Bess and George. "You're old high-school friends of Rachel's. When Mrs. Thackett answers the door, I'll duck down so she doesn't see me."

"Right," George and Bess chorused.

Nancy checked her watch. "It shouldn't take me very long. See you in ten minutes."

Nancy watched from the car as George and Bess walked up the steps to the front door. When they rang the bell, she bent low in the car seat.

Almost immediately Nancy heard the murmur of voices and the front door slamming shut. She waited a few seconds, then opened the car door on the side away from the house and slipped from the Mustang. The grounds were well landscaped, but since the leaves weren't out on the trees yet, Nancy had to be careful not to be seen.

She reached the garage in a few seconds and darted around the side, where she found a window. Rising on tiptoes, she peered inside. The blue sedan was parked closer to her, but next to it was a second car.

Nancy's heart skipped a beat.

It was a silver Mercedes!

Chapter

Eleven

So Mrs. Thackett's car might have been at the scene of the crime, Nancy thought. Or it could just be a coincidence. Hers certainly wasn't the only silver Mercedes in River Heights. Besides, she'd been seen at the theater. Could someone else have been driving her car?

Ducking low, Nancy made her way back to the Mustang, slid into the driver's seat, and settled down low. Bess and George did not return as quickly as Nancy had hoped, however. Her muscles were beginning to cramp when the front door of the Thacketts' house finally flew open.

"Goodbye! Thank you!" Nancy heard Bess and George call. Once Nancy heard the front door close behind her friends, she sat up. She quickly started the car as Bess and George jumped in.

"Whew," Bess gasped when they were halfway down the circular drive. "That woman is obsessed with her daughter."

"That's for sure," George agreed. "Mrs. Thackett has lived her life around Rachel. The house is a monument to her. Every wall has pictures of Rachel performing—"

"Ballet, horseback riding, gymnastics," Bess added, leaning on the back of George's seat. "She even brought out the photo albums." Bess rolled her eyes. "Honestly, if we hadn't told her we had a lunch date, we would have been there all day."

"It's no wonder Rachel split," George said. "If my mom acted like that, I'd feel totally smothered."

"Did she say anything about where Rachel was?" Nancy asked.

George and Bess exchanged glances. "She told us Rachel was in New York, visiting friends," George said.

"Even though I knew she was lying, I felt sorry for her," Bess added.

"Don't feel too sorry. There's a silver Mercedes in her garage," Nancy told them.

Bess gasped. "You mean *she* killed Paul?"

"No, it means a car the same make as hers drove onto that field by the tracks."

George whistled. "Sounds like pretty solid evidence to me."

"Only if the police can prove it was the same

car," Nancy said. "If B.D. gets a warrant, they can scrape the tires for mud samples and compare it to the dirt around the tracks." She turned the car onto Main Street. "Look for a phone booth. I need to call B.D., then let's head to the teen center and see if Rachel's called."

"Tony would have tried to contact you," Bess said. "He's *very* responsible."

"*And* good-looking, smart, sensitive . . ." George teased her cousin.

Bess rapped her on the arm. "I hadn't noticed," she stated firmly. "After all, I'm still dating Kyle." Dropping her chin onto her arms, she sighed dejectedly. "Until he leaves in three days."

"Three days!" Nancy exclaimed.

Bess nodded. "Yeah. He's taking the job right away. Although I really think he just wants to get out in the sun and surf and date California girls."

"Oh, come on, Bess," George scoffed. "Kyle's really serious when it comes to his career. Besides, *you* were the one who said you should date other people."

"True."

"Hey, there's a phone booth." George pointed at a gas station. Nancy flicked on her turn signal.

"After you call, why don't we look for a place to grab a burger?" Bess suggested. "My stomach is telling me it's lunchtime."

"It's a deal." Nancy parked, then jumped out

of the car. She dialed B.D.'s number at the police station. He answered right away, and she told him about the Mercedes.

When Nancy got back into the car, Bess and George looked at her expectantly.

"B.D. says he'll have someone do more checking into Mrs. Thackett's alibi. If the police find out she was lying, they can get a warrant to search her garage. He also said he has two officers combing the area around Billie's apartment. So far there's no sign of Rachel."

George sighed. "Let's just hope Tony has good news."

After they picked up lunch from a drive-in, Nancy drove to the teen center. When they entered the hotline office, Tony looked up from a psychology text he was reading.

"Exam tomorrow," he told them as he shut the book. "Usually, the machine is on from twelve to three, but since I'm hanging around anyway, I thought I'd answer calls. It's been pretty quiet, though."

"Did Rachel call this morning?" Nancy asked.

He shook his head. "Sorry."

"No word from Rachel?" came a voice from the doorway. It was Mr. A. His face was flushed from the climb up the steps, and he was clutching a file folder stuffed with papers.

Nancy shook her head. "No. And nothing about the money we found hidden on the third floor."

"Well, keep me posted." He started to go, then hesitated. "Nancy, may I speak with you for a second?"

"Sure." Nancy joined him in the hallway.

"I've been trying to remember anything Paul might have done or said that might help with the case," he said, his voice low. "And I recall about a week or so ago, Paul was telling me more about meeting Rachel at the community college. Apparently, she had told him her mom had lots of money, but she didn't care about it."

"I figured Mrs. Thackett was pretty wealthy," Nancy commented.

The teen center director looked at her sharply and went on. "A few days later, when we were working in the office, Paul mentioned that he wanted to go to the University of Illinois next year, but that the tuition was too high. Then he jokingly said, 'But now that I've got Rachel, I don't have to worry about money anymore.'"

Nancy's eyes widened. "Thanks, Mr. A. Maybe that explains where the five thousand came from."

"Anytime." He patted her arm, then went down the stairs. Still standing in the middle of the hall, Nancy pondered what he had told her.

Would Rachel have given Paul the money? And if she had access to that much cash, why not rent her own apartment?

It didn't make sense, she decided. Still, she

tucked the information away as she returned to the hotline office.

"How about lunch? Everything's getting cold," Bess said, opening one of the bags and pulling out several wrapped burgers. "Tony? We got one for you. And french fries, too."

"Great. Thanks," Tony said, reaching for the food.

Sitting on the edge of the desk, Nancy unwrapped her burger. For the next ten minutes, they ate while they discussed the case. Then the phone rang. Nancy grabbed for it, hoping it was Rachel, but it was B.D.

"I'm down at the community theater," he told her. "And guess what. It didn't take long before I found an usher who saw Mrs. Thackett sneak out an exit about nine-thirty on Monday night."

"What!" Nancy's mouth dropped open.

"I'm on my way to the judge to get a warrant to check her car tires and search her house. It seems that Mrs. Thackett has some explaining to do."

"Wow." Nancy slowly hung up the phone. She told George, Tony, and Bess what B.D. had discovered.

"So, not only does she not have an alibi for the night Paul was murdered," Nancy said, "but she also lied to the police. That may just put her at the top of the suspect list. If she's as obsessed with Rachel as you say, maybe she got so angry at Paul for supposedly stealing her daughter away that she lost it."

"I don't know." Bess shook her head in disbelief. "I can't see Mrs. Thackett knifing someone. And even if Rachel witnessed it, Mrs. Thackett wouldn't go after her own daughter."

Nancy frowned. "Good point."

"Really. If you ask me, the whole thing doesn't seem like Mrs. Thackett's style," George said, biting into a french fry.

"I disagree," Tony cut in. "It sounds as if that lady has a 'control complex'—as they say in the psychology books. When Rachel defied her, she may have freaked out."

"Could be," Nancy said. "But I do have to agree with Bess and George—things just don't quite fit. If Mrs. Thackett wanted somebody killed she probably would have—" Suddenly the answer popped into her head. "That's it! Bossing someone around and paying him lots of money would be Mrs. Thackett's style, right?"

"Right," Bess agreed.

"So maybe she hired somebody to do the dirty work," Nancy said.

George slapped the desk. "I think you're right. Though if Mrs. Thackett hired someone to do the job, isn't she just as guilty?"

"Yes she is." The phone rang again. Deep in thought, Nancy wiped off her greasy fingers, then picked it up slowly. "Hello. Help Is Here Hotline. Nancy speaking."

"Nancy? It's Rachel."

Quickly, Nancy jumped off the desk and

grabbed a pad of paper. "Rachel? I'm so glad you called." Checking her watch, she noted the exact time so B.D. could cross-check the call with the phone company. Bess, George, and Tony stopped eating to listen.

"Are you okay?" Nancy continued.

"Yeah, I'm all right," Rachel said, but then she began to sob. "No, I'm not okay. I'm so worried and tired and hungry that I'm starting to freak out."

"Rachel, please let us help," Nancy pleaded. "Is there anything we can do for you?"

"Yes." Her voice was so soft, Nancy could barely hear her. "But only you. You're the only one I trust. The night Paul was murdered, he gave me an envelope. He said if something happened to him, I was supposed to get it to the police. But I want *you* to take it to them for me. Tonight, at ten o'clock, go to the alley behind Billie's apartment. I'll leave the envelope under the third trash can."

"Why are you afraid to go to the police yourself?" Nancy asked. A click told her that Rachel had hung up.

"Well?" George prompted.

Nancy explained about the envelope, then quickly called the police department and left a message for B.D. stating the time that Rachel had called. The phone company could then trace where the call had originated from, which would narrow the search for her.

After that, Nancy sat down on the edge of the desk again. "I'm stumped," she admitted. "What could possibly be in that envelope?"

"I don't know," Bess replied. "But we'll soon find out!"

At ten o'clock on the dot, Bess drove Nancy and George to Billie's apartment.

"Keep the motor running," Nancy suggested. "If everything goes okay, I'll be back in a second."

"Be careful," George said as Nancy shut the door of Bess's Camaro and headed down the dark alley beside the building.

Nancy had dressed in black and tucked her hair into a baseball cap in order to look as inconspicuous as possible. Once her eyes adjusted to the dark, she was able to move swiftly down the alley. Reaching the rear corner, she peered around the building. Six trash cans were lined up in a row by the back entrance. They were overflowing with garbage.

Nancy hesitated. Was the envelope under the third trash can from the right, or from the left?

Cautiously, she crept around the corner to the third can from the left. Bending down, she tilted it up. The lid fell off, and a smelly bag fell at her feet.

"Phew!" Nancy moved back, the same instant she heard soft footsteps behind her.

Instantly, she twirled around. A knife blade

slashed through the air, catching the sleeve of her jacket. She jumped sideways, fell over a trash can, and landed on an overstuffed plastic bag. Instinctively, she raised one hand to shield herself from the attacker before glancing up.

Standing over her was a figure wearing a ski mask and a black leather jacket with an *N* on the front. In one fist a knife blade gleamed in the moonlight.

Nancy screamed as the attacker stepped toward her, ready to strike again!

Chapter
Twelve

USING ALL HER STRENGTH, Nancy kicked the trash can beside her, toppling it into the black figure's knees. For a second her assailant staggered backward, giving her time to scramble to her feet. But before she could run, the attacker lunged at Nancy. As she dodged the glistening blade, her heart pounded like a drum. How long could she hold him off?

Suddenly, a bloodcurdling yell came from Nancy's right. The attacker froze for an instant, glanced to the left, then spun around and raced off in the opposite direction. The attacker turned the corner and disappeared. Bess and George had rounded the other corner of the building. Hands cupped around her mouth, Bess let out another piercing yell.

"Nancy! Are you all right?" George asked, rushing up to her friend.

Nancy stepped over the fallen trash can and garbage. "Yes. Thanks to you guys."

"We heard you scream," Bess explained. "I know we weren't supposed to leave the car, but—"

"That's all right." Grinning, Nancy gave Bess a hug. "Where did you learn to yell like that?"

"Self-defense class."

George bent down to help Nancy pick up the trash can. "From what I could see, that guy meant business." Concerned, she glanced at Nancy. "Where did he come from? We didn't see him go into the alley."

"He could've come from the other side," Nancy said. "This back alley leads out to another street."

"Was that a knife he was holding?" Bess asked.

Nancy nodded. "And he had a black jacket with an *N* on the front."

"Like the ones the Nighthawks wear?" Bess's eyes widened.

"Right." Nancy turned and quickly found the third trash can from the right. She pulled it away from the building wall. "And I have a feeling whoever it was was after this." Bending down, she picked up a white standard-size envelope that had been under the trash can. She held it up. "Luckily, I checked under the wrong can at first. Otherwise, the attacker would have gotten it."

Bess and George gathered around Nancy. Silently, all three stared at the envelope.

"Well, are you going to open it?" George finally asked.

"Hey, guys, let's go somewhere safe first," Bess said, nervously looking around. "The attacker may have friends. Like a whole gang of them."

The three made sure all the trash was picked up, then ran back to the Camaro. After the car doors were locked, Nancy opened the envelope. Inside was a paper folded in thirds.

"Let me guess," Bess said excitedly. "It's a note telling the police who killed Paul."

Nancy pulled it out and unfolded it. A smaller piece of paper fell to her lap. "No. It's a page from an account ledger and a check."

"Huh?" George grabbed the larger paper from Nancy. "Accounts payable. Accounts receivable. You're right. What's on the check?"

"It's for a thousand dollars and written out to the teen center. And it's signed by a lady named Johnson."

"A donation?" Bess guessed. "That's weird. Let me see that page from the account book."

George handed the paper to Bess, who held it up to the light coming in the window. Squinting, she scrutinized both sides. "I'll bet there's a message written on it in invisible ink. What do you think, Nan?"

Taking the paper, Nancy refolded it and put it back in the envelope with the check. "I think the more important question is: How did the attacker find out I was picking up that envelope?" She looked directly at George, then at Bess. "Did either of you tell a soul where we were going tonight?"

They both shook their heads.

Nancy rubbed her chin. "What if the attacker wasn't after the envelope? What if he or she thought I was Rachel?"

"You mean the person could have been after Rachel, not the envelope?" Bess asked in a whisper. "To—to kill her?"

Nancy frowned. "Let's hope not."

"Maybe we were followed." George spun around in the car seat and looked out the back window.

Bess shook her head. "No way. I would have noticed."

"It could be that someone's watching the apartment house all the time, hoping to catch Rachel, or—" Nancy paused. Leaning back in the seat, she thought a second. "Or the phone at the hotline is bugged."

George and Bess exchanged puzzled glances.

"It already is—by the phone company," George reminded Nancy.

"That's different. They don't listen in on the conversations. I mean *really* bugged by whoever wants to catch Rachel." Nancy tapped Bess on the shoulder. "Let's head to the teen center. The last hotline shift isn't over yet, so we should be able to get in."

"You got it," Bess said firmly as she started up the car and stepped on the gas. The Camaro squealed away from the curb. Fifteen minutes later the girls ran upstairs and into the hotline office.

Startled, Tony's head jerked upright. His feet were propped on the desk, and he was still reading his psychology text.

"Slow night?" Bess asked.

He nodded. "Yeah, I let the volunteers go a little early. But from the flushed looks on your faces, I'd say things are just about to get more exciting."

"That's for sure," Nancy said.

He shot her a puzzled look. When the girls finished telling him all that had happened, he whistled softly. "Do you think Paul stole the check from the center?"

"I don't know," Nancy replied. "If he'd found a way to cash teen center donation checks, that would account for the five thousand he had stashed in his room. But then why would he give the check to Rachel to hand over to the police? It would only prove he was guilty of stealing." She shook her head in confusion, then reached for the phone receiver. "Anyway, right now I want to check these phones. If someone has bugged them, we may be putting Rachel in jeopardy."

Unscrewing the cap on the end of the receiver, she checked inside.

"It's clean." She screwed the receiver back together, replaced it on the phone, and checked the second one. "Nothing. Which means it must be tapped along the line somewhere."

"So what should we look for?" Bess asked.

Nancy snapped her fingers. "Wait a minute. I remember a case where the main phone line was bugged. It was in an old building like this one, and the main connection panel was in the basement."

She swung her gaze to Tony. "Does this place have a basement?"

"Yeah. But I've never been down there."

Nancy pulled her flashlight from her purse. "There's always a first time."

"Bess and I will answer the phones until the hotline closes," George said.

"Are you sure you know what you're doing?" Tony asked Nancy as they went down to the first floor.

Nancy laughed. "No. But I'll figure it out as I go."

She followed him past the rec room and Mr. A's office. The door was closed, and the only light still on was the one in the hallway.

"The basement," Tony said, pointing to the door beyond the director's office.

Slowly, he opened it. A wave of damp, musty air hit Nancy in the face.

Tony ran his fingers along the wall, looking for a light switch. When he flicked it on, nothing happened.

"Great," he muttered. "This could be a scene from a horror movie."

Nancy grinned, pulled her flashlight out of her bag, then flicked it on. The beam lighted the wooden steps and the landing at the bottom. Cobwebs hung from the banister.

"I'll go first." Nancy stepped onto the top step. It creaked eerily. Carefully, she made her way down into the dungeonlike room. She could hear Tony's footsteps behind her.

When she reached the bottom, she swung the beam in an arc. Shadows loomed in every corner. A lone light socket hung from the ceiling. Nancy aimed the flashlight on it.

"Someone took the bulb out," she whispered.

Nervously, Tony stepped closer to her. "Let's just hope whoever took it isn't big and mean—and still here."

"Look!" Nancy pointed the beam at the wall on the right. Next to the furnace was the main phone panel, the box where all the phone lines in the building converged.

Nancy scrambled over several dust-covered boxes to get to it. From the panel, a number of colored wires ran in different directions.

"What are we looking for?" Tony asked.

"Other wires spliced into these colored ones," Nancy told him. "That means someone has tapped directly into the line. In newer buildings, the phone wiring is in a secured area. But in these old buildings it's wide open—a wiretapper's dream."

"Boy, this is more like a spy movie than a horror film." Tony moved to Nancy's right and began checking the wires that went toward the ceiling. Bending down, Nancy ran her fingers along the ones that headed behind the furnace.

"Bingo!" she said triumphantly. She aimed her flashlight on a wire that had been cut in two. New wires had been taped onto each end of the cut wire. Nancy ran the flashlight beam down the spliced-on wires, following them all the way to a tape recorder concealed in a shoebox behind the furnace.

"Whew." Nancy whistled appreciatively. "Someone knows what they're doing. I bet the recorder has a dropout relay. That means when the phone is used, the recorder automatically switches on."

Tony peered over Nancy's shoulder, trying to get a better look. "So how do we know if it works?"

"We try it out. Go up to the pay phone and call the hotline number. I'll stay here and see if the tape recorder starts up."

Tony looked uncertain. "You're going to stay down here—alone?"

"Sure." Nancy gave him a reassuring smile.

"I'll be fine. Once we know if this works, we'll call B.D."

"All right."

Stepping away from the furnace, Nancy turned her flashlight toward the steps so Tony could see where he was going. He stumbled over a box, then hurried up the stairs.

Nancy had to chuckle. She couldn't blame him for wanting to get out of the basement as quickly as possible. Crouching down, she pushed her way behind the furnace as close to the recorder as she could get. Then she aimed the beam of light onto the tape inside the recorder. There probably wouldn't be any sound, so she'd have to watch and see if the reels were activated.

While she waited, she wondered who could have bugged the lines. Since anyone could come into the center, the suspects were limitless, although it did have to be someone who had knowledge of wiretapping and knew there was a basement.

And someone who desperately wanted to find Rachel—which meant whoever set up the recorder was probably Paul's killer.

Nancy was deep in thought when she heard a creak on the top step. Startled, she jerked upright, then held her breath to listen.

The basement was silent.

Nancy clicked off her flashlight, plunging the room into darkness. A moment later she saw a beam of light at the top of the stairs. Her heart pounded with fear as she watched the light dancing on the steps.

Someone was coming down the stairs, slowly and furtively. Nancy's breath caught in her throat as a terrible thought shot through her mind.

It could be Paul's murderer!

Chapter

Thirteen

NANCY GRIPPED her own flashlight tightly. She had to find a hiding place.

Quickly, she racked her brain, trying to remember what the rest of the basement looked like. An image of boxes stacked on the far side of the furnace flashed into her mind.

As the beam of light moved downward, it faintly illuminated the basement. Nancy could see the dark shape of the boxes.

Ducking low, she crept from behind the dusty furnace. Then she flattened herself on the floor and inched her way behind a wide box on the other side.

Just in time.

The beam of light swung toward the furnace, then in the direction of the tape recorder. Nancy held her breath. Whoever was in the basement had to have been the person who bugged the phone!

Nancy heard a click. She peered around the box, trying to get a glimpse of the person's face. But the furnace was in the way.

Then the light swung back toward the steps, and moving swiftly, the person made his or her way upstairs. Nancy jumped up, but all she could see were two shadowy feet disappearing up the steps. Then she heard the door close.

Snapping on her own flashlight, Nancy pushed past the boxes. When she reached the furnace, she aimed her light on the tape recorder. The person had taken the reel of tape!

"Just great," Nancy muttered. Turning, she tiptoed upstairs. Maybe she could catch a glimpse of whoever it was.

When she reached the top step, she paused. She heard the footsteps in the hallway. Quickly, she banged open the door.

"Ow!" The door caught Tony on the elbow. "What's going on?" he asked when he saw her face.

"Did you see anyone?" Nancy asked as she glanced down the hall to the foyer.

"No. Why?"

Without answering, Nancy raced to the front door, which was slightly ajar. But when she jerked it open and ran outside, there was no one on the sidewalk or street.

"What's going on?" Tony asked from the doorway. He was staring at her, a puzzled expression on his face.

"Someone came down into the basement and took the tape," Nancy said as she came back inside. "Was anyone around when you came upstairs?"

"No. But since I was on the phone in the rec room, I couldn't see," Tony explained.

Nancy blew out her breath. "Then we lost him—or her. It does tell us one thing, though. Whoever bugged the phones knows when the hotline closes down. That must be why the person took the tape. He or she knew Rachel wouldn't call after eleven."

Turning, Nancy headed up the stairs. "We'd better tell Bess and George what happened."

"And I need to lock up the hotline office," Tony said, following her.

When they got upstairs, Kyle was sitting on the edge of Bess's desk, talking to her. From the expression on his face, Nancy could tell they'd been discussing something important.

"Hi, Kyle," Nancy said. "You didn't happen to see anyone dash out of the teen center when you came in, did you?"

"No, why?" Kyle asked.

Nancy and Tony told Bess, George, and Kyle all that had happened.

"Whew." Kyle rubbed his chin. "You guys do have exciting nights. Bess was telling me all about the guy in the leather jacket at the trash cans." He looked pointedly at Bess. "At least that's why she said she forgot to call me."

Nancy looked over at her friend, who had flushed pink. Then Nancy laughed. "Yeah, that's why she didn't call you. She was too busy driving the getaway car."

Kyle stood up and reached for Bess's hand. "Well, let's see if we can fit in a romantic late dinner before I take you home. After all, we only have a few more days together. Let's make the most of them."

"Sounds great." Bess grabbed her jacket from the back of the chair. She pulled her keys from her purse and tossed them to Nancy. "Just leave my car in your drive, Nan. And call me in the morning to let me know what happened."

When the two left, George turned her attention to Nancy. "So who do you think bugged the phone?"

"Someone who knows his or her way around the center," Nancy replied, suppressing a yawn. "Listen, guys, it's late. I'll have to call B.D. from home and tell him what happened. First the attacker, then the envelope, and now the phone bug—this case is getting more complicated every minute!"

An hour later Nancy was sprawled on her bed, studying the page from the account ledger. She'd showered and changed into her nightgown, but still she couldn't sleep. There were too many unanswered questions.

What was Paul trying to tell the police with the page from the ledger? she wondered. Nancy scanned the sheet, looking for answers. Most of the entries in the columns were abbreviated. There was no heading saying where the page had come from, and although the entries were dated for December and January, there wasn't a year. For all she knew, it was an assignment from one of Paul's business courses.

Setting down the page, Nancy glanced at her bedside phone. She wished B.D. would call. She'd left a message for him a half hour ago.

With a frustrated sigh, Nancy picked up the check for one thousand dollars. It had to be a donation to the teen center, she decided. Had Paul been stealing checks? And if so, why had he told Rachel to give this one to the police?

Suddenly it hit Nancy. What if Paul had a partner, and the two of them had been embezzling money from the center? Only something went wrong—the partner got greedy or Paul decided to quit the scam—so the partner decided to kill him. That's why Paul had given Rachel the check. If he was killed, it might tip off the police about the identity of his murderer.

The partner would have to be someone who was streetwise enough to know how to sneak into the center and bug a phone.

Someone like Kip DiFranco.

Nancy's mind buzzed excitedly. It all made sense. If Kip and Paul's partnership had gone sour, maybe that was one reason Paul ratted on Kip about the burglary. If so, Kip would have had *two* reasons to murder Paul.

Nancy glanced at the phone again. "Hurry and call, B.D.," she whispered aloud.

Then another question hit her. If Kip was the murderer, how did the page from the account ledger fit in?

Nancy held the sheet up to the light. Maybe it *did* bear a message in invisible ink, as Bess had suggested. She turned it over. In the left-hand corner, she saw numbers written lightly in pencil.

Sitting up, she pulled out the drawer of her bedside table and reached for her magnifying glass. When she looked at the paper under the glass, a series of numbers jumped out at her— 1287028216. After the numbers someone had printed "Chicago B & T."

Nancy got up and padded downstairs to her father's office. She switched on the light, then went directly to his bookshelf where he kept a pile of phone books. She pulled out the heavy book for the Chicago area and opened it on his desk. Turning to the listings that began with Chicago, she ran her finger down the page. The answer leapt out at her—Chicago Bank and Trust!

Nancy glanced down again at the numbers on

the back of the page from the ledger. They had to be an account number, she told herself excitedly.

The phone rang next to her. Nancy reached for the receiver. "Hello?"

"Hi, Nancy, this is B.D. I got a message that you called."

"B.D.," Nancy said breathlessly, "wait until you hear my news! I think I just found the evidence you need to crack this case."

B.D. chuckled. "Slow down. We may both have cracked the case."

"What do you mean?" Nancy asked. "What did you find out?"

"You tell me your information first."

"Okay." After taking a deep breath, Nancy launched into her tale about the attacker, finding the envelope, and locating the tape recorder.

"Wow. You really were busy," B.D. said. "That was good work finding that phone bug. My hunch is we shouldn't disturb it. I'll see if I can get an officer to watch the center. We may be able to nab our culprit trying to put in a new tape."

"Good. And there's more," Nancy continued. "There was a check made out to the teen center and a page from an account ledger in the envelope. I figured out that the check was an uncashed donation to the center." Nancy told the detective her hunch about Paul and a partner working together. "What if the partnership soured?" she added. "Paul might have decided to go straight. Or the partner got greedy, so he killed Paul."

"Uh-huh. And who might this fictitious partner be?" B.D. asked.

"Kip DiFranco, of course, which means you were right all along." Nancy told him all the reasons why Kip was a likely suspect.

"Hmmm." There was silence on the other end. "So maybe Paul was about to double-cross Kip a second time by taking his information about the scam to the police?"

Nancy nodded. "Right. But all this is just speculation. I found one more clue that may finger our killer for sure. Written on the page from the ledger was an account number and the name of a bank—Chicago Bank and Trust. I'll bet if you can trace the holder of that account, we'll have the name of our killer!"

Chapter

Fourteen

GOOD WORK, DETECTIVE DREW!" B.D. said on the other end of the phone. "Give me the account number. I should have a name for you by the morning."

"Now, what's your information?" Nancy asked eagerly.

"This evening the lab confirmed that the mud from Mrs. Thackett's car and a sample of mud from the scene of the crime are a definite match," B.D. said. "Plus, we just finished questioning Mrs. Thackett. At first she was pretty cooperative, then we told her about the usher seeing her leaving the theater. Well, she quickly clammed up and called some high-powered lawyer. But before she did, we found out one interesting piece of news." B.D. paused. "That money stashed in Paul's room? It was a payoff from Rachel's dear mother."

"You mean Mrs. Thackett paid Paul *not* to see her daughter?" Nancy gasped.

"Right. My guess is Paul met Rachel's mother at the warehouse to tell her he was keeping the money and that he was still going to see her daughter. Might be motive enough for murder, don't you think?"

"Might be." Nancy frowned. "And that blows my whole theory about Paul's money coming from stolen checks."

B.D. chuckled. "Yeah. I knew you'd be disappointed. Still, I'll find out about that account number, so you be down at the police station first thing in the morning."

"Don't worry," Nancy said, suppressing a huge yawn. "I will."

"The account belongs to J. R. Communications," B.D. told her the next morning. It was nine-thirty, and Nancy was standing in front of the detective's desk. B.D. was leaning back in his swivel chair, his feet in their cowboy boots propped up on the top of his desk. His brown hair was pulled back in a short ponytail.

"J. R. Communications? Who's that?"

B.D. shrugged. "Some company. They have a post office box number in Chicago, but they're not listed in the directory."

With a frustrated groan, Nancy sat down on a chair in front of the desk. "And I was so sure that account belonged to the killer."

"It's never that easy." B.D. chuckled. "But I think with a little more evidence, we'll be able to arrest Mrs. Thackett."

"You mean evidence like Rachel fingering her own mother?" Nancy asked.

"Right. Which brings me to the really good news—we traced the phone number to a booth on Fourteenth and Main Street. Early this morning, two of my men located a clerk at a hotel near that intersection who thinks Rachel might be staying there. They're waiting for the manager, to see if he can ID her. They should be calling in any minute."

Nancy's eyes brightened. "Can I come with you?"

"Yes. I want you there since Rachel seems to trust you. We need to get her into the station, take her statement, and close this case." B.D. pounded one hand on the desk for emphasis.

Outside B.D.'s office, phones rang, and police officers bustled back and forth, but Nancy didn't notice any of it. "B.D., if Mrs. Thackett's the murderer, then how do you explain the *N* slashed on Paul's shirt? And what about the person in black who attacked me and the phone-bugging and the stuff in the envelope?" Nancy shook her head. "If you ask me, it doesn't add up."

"You're right," B.D. agreed. "But my job is to take the evidence and make the best sense out of it I can."

Nancy frowned and, making a steeple with her fingers, rested her chin on them. "That's what I'm trying to do, too. You know one of my theories was that Mrs. Thackett hired someone to help her. I figured—"

B.D. dropped his feet onto the floor and let out a whoop. "That's it, Drew!" He jumped up. "There are tons of private detectives out there who'd do anything for a buck. I'm going to get some officers on it. If we can prove that Mrs. Thackett hired someone to do her dirty work, we'll really nail her!"

Before Nancy could say anything, he gave her the thumbs-up sign and strode from the office.

When he left, Nancy's frown only deepened. A hired detective still didn't explain the information in the envelope.

Reaching into her jacket pocket, Nancy slid out the envelope and reread the name and address on the check. The address was for a posh area in River Heights. Nancy had assumed the thousand-dollar check was a donation. But what if it wasn't?

There was one easy way to find out. Nancy got up and hunted around B.D.'s office until she found a local phone book. Then she looked up Mrs. Johnson's number and dialed.

"Hello. Mrs. Johnson? This is Nancy Drew from the teen center."

"The teen center!" The woman chirped on the other end. "What a wonderful place. What can I do for you, Miss Drew?"

"We wanted to thank you for your generous donation," Nancy replied.

"Oh, there's no need to thank me," Mrs. Johnson gushed. "Thank *you* for all the fine work you folks do at the center. I know my checks for December and January funded some excellent projects. So you tell Mr. A that if he keeps up that wonderful work, my next check will arrive right on time!"

Nancy thanked her, then said goodbye.

She looked at the check again. It was dated February 24. Last month. And Mrs. Johnson had already sent checks for December and January.

Hmmm. December and January were the months covered in the accounting ledger.

Could there be a connection?

Slim chance, Nancy thought, still—

She unfolded the ledger page and scanned the columns. On the accounts payable side someone had written "nls, lmbr, sw, hmmr, Shtrk," then a monetary amount.

Nancy studied the abbreviations. If you added vowels, the words were *nails, lumber, saw, hammer, Sheetrock,* items that had been bought for the renovation of the dorm in the teen center.

A prickle of excitement raced up Nancy's spine. Was the page from a teen center ledger? If Paul and Kip were partners in some kind of financial scam, what better place to embezzle money from than the teen center? Mr. A had said Paul helped with the paperwork, so he probably had had access to the books.

Nancy grabbed a piece of scrap paper, and started writing down the first four entries in the accounts receivable column, adding vowels as she listed them: Henry Dorset and Family—$2,000; Lions Club—$1,240; G. D. Hopkins—$400; Women's Auxiliary—$560.

It had to be a list of donors, Nancy decided. That meant the page could definitely be from the teen center account ledger!

Quickly, she added up the sums in the accounts receivable column. In two months, the center had taken in over ten thousand dollars in donations. Yet, adding up the accounts payable side showed that the center had spent only two thousand dollars in that same period of time.

Where was the other eight thousand dollars? Nancy wondered. Was Mr. A saving it for the new dorm? Except, when they'd been on the third floor, she clearly remembered the director telling her that funds had dried up.

Again, Nancy studied the accounting page. She made another discovery: Mrs. Johnson's donations for December and January weren't listed on the sheet!

Nancy reached for the phone and dialed Mrs. Johnson. "Excuse me for bothering you again," she said. "But did we send you a receipt for your donation?"

"Receipt? Oh, that's not necessary," Mrs. Johnson replied. "That's what I told that fine young man when I gave him the last check."

"You mean Paul?" Nancy asked, her mouth going dry.

"Why, yes. I told him that the best receipt the center could give me was the assurance that my money was helping send some poor child to college."

"Thank you," Nancy said politely. Only I think your money was helping some crook get rich, she thought. Someone could even have stolen checks right out of the teen center mailbox.

Just then B.D. burst into his office. "Mission accomplished. I've got two guys ready to shake down every private eye in the area."

"Great, B.D.," Nancy said. "Only look at this." She held out the page from the ledger. "I think I've finally figured out what Paul was trying to tell us."

"What's that?" B.D.'s brow furrowed as he glanced down at the sheet she was holding out. But when Nancy started to explain about the missing donations, he strolled around his desk, sat down, and propped his feet up again.

"Look, Nancy," he finally interrupted. "From

what I'm hearing, someone *was* probably stealing checks from the center, and maybe there was a little creative accounting going on, too. But that's a job for the fraud unit. This is a murder investigation."

"I know, but this all ties into my hunch that Paul was working with a partner who—"

The phone rang on B.D.'s desk, cutting Nancy off.

"Detective Hawkins," B.D. answered. "Yeah." As he listened, the detective's eyes flashed excitedly, and he dropped his feet to the floor. "We'll be there in five minutes." Grinning, he slammed down the phone. "Let's roll," he told Nancy as he jumped up and grabbed his jacket from the hook on the wall. "They've found Rachel!"

Ten minutes later B.D. pulled to the curb in front of the Chestmont Hotel. As Nancy climbed out, two plainclothes officers immediately approached the car. While B.D. talked with them, Nancy studied the hotel. It was a narrow, three-story brick structure with ornate molding and cornices that told her it had once been quite grand. Now the paint was peeling, and the bricks were gray with soot.

"She's in room 3B," B.D. told Nancy. Taking her arm, he escorted her into the lobby of the hotel. "Both the day clerk and the manager have identified her."

As they climbed the stairs, Nancy's heart

pounded with excitement. When they reached the third floor, B.D. directed one officer to stand in front of the stairs and the other officer to wait at the end of the hall.

"Okay, Nancy. This is where you do your thing," B.D. said, pointing to 3B.

Nancy nodded, took a deep breath, then rapped on the door. "Rachel?" she called. "It's Nancy from the hotline."

When there was no answer, Nancy pressed her ear to the door. "Rachel? I know you're in there. And I know you're scared. Let me help. Please."

This time Nancy heard shuffling sounds, as if someone was walking slowly to the door.

"Nancy?" a voice whispered.

"Hi, Rachel." Nancy tried to sound cheery. "Won't you let me in?"

There was a long silence. Then Nancy heard the sound of a deadbolt turning. She glanced up at B.D. He nodded, then flattened himself against the left side of the door.

The door opened a couple of inches. Rachel peered through the crack. Nancy could see that the girl's red hair was a tangled mass of curls and that her eyes were bloodshot. "Are you alone?" Rachel asked.

Nancy gulped. She knew if she lied, she might lose Rachel's trust. "No. But—"

Before the door could slam shut, Nancy stuck

her foot in the crack. Then B.D. whirled to her side and shoved the door open with both hands.

Rachel fell backward onto the bed. With a cry of pain, she raised her arms in front of her face as if to shield herself from a blow.

"It's all right!" Nancy rushed to the girl's side, slid her arm around her shoulders and held her close. "This is Detective Hawkins, Rachel. He's here to help you."

B.D. leaned down. "Hey. I'm a good guy." He grinned at her.

Lowering her arms, Rachel laid her head on Nancy's shoulder and started to cry with exhaustion. Nancy hugged her closer, then glanced around the tiny room. The bed took up most of one side. On the other side was a narrow closet, and next to it, a door leading into a bathroom. The bedroom had a window that opened to a fire escape.

"I'm sorry," Rachel sobbed. "I guess I really am glad to see you. I thought I was doing the right thing, but—now I'm so tired and hungry and confused, I don't know what I'm doing."

B.D. jumped up and waved to the officer in the hallway. "Get us something hot and nourishing to eat. Soup, tea, whatever. And make it quick," he called, then sat down on the other side of Rachel. "Hey. You need to quit running and let us help. That's what we're here for."

"I know." Rachel sniffed. Nancy pulled a tissue from her pocket and handed it to her.

Rachel wiped her cheeks, then blew her nose. "Only I'm not running from the police," she whispered. "I'm running from that night. From that horrible nightmare. Because—" She shuddered and her eyes filled with tears. "I saw my mother kill Paul!"

Chapter

Fifteen

"YOU ACTUALLY SAW your mother kill Paul?" Nancy exclaimed.

Rachel dabbed her freckled cheeks with the tissue. "No. But I know who it was. Paul came to Billie's apartment on Monday night. He was really upset. He said he had a meeting with someone at ten o'clock. When he said it was by the warehouse, I got really worried because that's where the members of his old gang hang out."

She gulped, then went on. "But I didn't have a car, so I had to call a cab. By the time I made it to the back of the warehouse, all I saw was my mother standing over the body. The headlights of her car were on, so I saw her clearly."

She looked up at B.D., then at Nancy, tears filling her eyes again. "I knew she wanted to kill Paul. She hated him because she thought he was the reason I wouldn't come home. She'd already tried to pay him off with five thousand dollars!"

Rachel's shoulders stiffened. "Monday morning I went up to Paul's room. He showed me the money. I couldn't believe it! For eighteen years she's run my life as if I were a prize show dog. Now she was trying to pay off the first guy who ever liked me just for myself." She gave Nancy a sad smile. "Paul told me he was giving the money back to her."

Then abruptly, she stood up, her cheeks flushed with anger. "So when he came over to Billie's apartment that night, I figured it was her he was meeting behind the warehouse. When he gave her back the money and told her he was still going to see me, she must've been so furious she killed him!"

Her arms wrapped protectively around her, Rachel looked first at Nancy, then at B.D. with an expression of despair. "I knew my mother would do anything to get me away from Paul, but I didn't think she'd kill him."

"Why didn't you call the police?" B.D. asked.

"I couldn't turn in my own mother!" Rachel exclaimed. "I knew I had to report the murder, so I called the hotline, hoping Billie was on duty and she'd know what to do. When Nancy answered, I panicked and ran." Her shoulders slumped. Turning, she stared vacantly out the window. "Only now—now I see that if my mother's guilty, she has to be punished."

133

B.D. slapped his hand on his thigh. "Well, case closed," he announced.

A rap on the door announced the arrival of Rachel's food. Minutes later, she was sitting on the edge of the bed, wolfing down a ham sandwich, french fries, and a chocolate milk shake. B.D. was perched on the windowsill, eating a hamburger.

When Rachel finally leaned back on the bed with a satisfied sigh, Nancy asked the questions that had been bothering her.

"Rachel, why do you think Paul gave you that envelope for the police? And when did he give it to you?"

"Monday night, when he came over to Billie's apartment. He told me about the meeting, then handed me the envelope. He said to give it to the cops if something happened."

"Did you know what was in it?" Nancy asked.

"Look, Nan," B.D. said as he threw his trash away. "Let's get Rachel down to the station where we can do this officially. She's got a lot of questions to answer."

Nancy jumped up. "Wait, B.D. If Paul gave Rachel the page from the teen center account and the check and told her to go to the police if anything happened to him, then it has to have *something* to do with why he was murdered."

Nancy swung her gaze to Rachel. "Was your mother in any way involved with the teen center? Did she ever make a donation?"

Rachel snorted. "No way. My mother hates any kids who don't look like they're headed to Harvard."

"See?" Nancy grabbed B.D.'s arm. "There's more to this case than Rachel's mom. Paul must have found out that something shady was going on at the center. Maybe he was even in on it, but then changed his mind."

B.D. looked unconvinced. "You already explained all that, Nancy. But now that we have Rachel's testimony, my job is to arrest Mrs. Thackett for Paul's murder."

"But what if there's a chance the killer *isn't* Mrs. Thackett?"

B.D. crossed his arms and gave Nancy a wary look. "All right. What do you have in mind?"

"Since the phone tap and the tape recorder are still hooked up, we need to have Rachel call the hotline and tell the volunteer where she is."

Now Rachel looked confused. "But you already know where I am."

"Only B.D. and I know," Nancy explained. "Whoever tapped the phone has obviously been looking for you, too. My hunch is when the real killer hears the message on the tape recorder, he or she will rush over here, pronto!"

"And we'll nab him." B.D. suddenly looked interested.

Even Rachel brightened. "I'll do anything to help, especially if there's a chance the murderer isn't my mother."

"No. You've done enough." Nancy touched Rachel lightly on the hand. "I'll stay here and pretend I'm you."

B.D. jerked his head up. "No way, Drew. You've done some crazy things before, but the police department has trained officers for situations like this."

"Only there's no time to get one up here and brief her," Nancy protested. "Besides, you'll be here to protect me," she added, smiling convincingly.

B.D. rolled his eyes. "Oh, boy. Why do I let you talk me into these things?"

"Because you know I'm right," Nancy teased. "Come on, Rachel, let's make that call, then we'll switch clothes."

An hour later Nancy was crouched behind the closed bathroom door. She had the water running in the sink as if she were washing up. B.D. was hiding in the tiny closet, his gun drawn, the door cracked open.

Nancy was glad that Rachel was safe at the police station. She was also glad B.D. had gone along with her plan. She knew that he had enough information to arrest Mrs. Thackett. And since they'd been waiting an hour and no one had shown up, she was beginning to think he was right—that the bookkeeping page and the check in the envelope weren't related to the murder.

Nancy grimaced as she rubbed a cramp in her

left calf. Then she stuck a finger under the red wig she was wearing and scratched her scalp. Lucky for her, one of the undercover cops at the station had had it in his locker and was able to bring it over.

Suddenly, the bedroom door opened with such a loud bang, Nancy almost fell over.

"Rachel!" Mrs. Thackett's voice boomed through the room. "Thank goodness I—"

Her voice was abruptly cut off by the sound of B.D. charging from the closet and yelling, "Halt! You're under arrest for the murder of Paul Remer!"

Mrs. Thackett screamed.

For a second Nancy was stunned. So Rachel's mother *had* killed Paul. Slowly, she stood up. She could hear Mrs. Thackett protesting shrilly.

When she went out into the room, B.D. was handcuffing the woman. Two other officers had rushed to the doorway when Mrs. Thackett screamed.

"I want my lawyer," Mrs. Thackett was now demanding loudly. "You police have harassed me enough. Take these handcuffs off, right now."

"Lady, if you were innocent, you wouldn't be here," B.D. said. He handed her over to the tall officer. "Read Mrs. Thackett her rights, then take her down to your squad car. I'll be with you in a second."

Still complaining noisily, Mrs. Thackett was led out the door.

"Well, Nancy, can we finally close this case?" B.D. asked her.

She nodded. "Yes. Still, it's hard to believe Mrs. Thackett hated Paul enough to kill him."

"Let's just say she loved her daughter too much," B.D. replied, shaking his head. "And you may be right. She might have hired someone who researched Paul's background and knew he'd had a run-in with the Nighthawks." He sighed. "I'm sure the whole story will come out soon enough."

"Yes, but I sure feel sorry for Rachel," Nancy said. "She's been through a lot, and now there's even more in store for her."

"I know. Can I give you a lift?"

Nancy glanced around the tiny room. She'd noticed some of Rachel's things in the bathroom. "Let me just get Rachel's stuff, and and I'll be down."

B.D. smiled, then left the room.

Nancy started toward the bathroom doorway. A loud *thunk* outside the bedroom window made her freeze in her tracks. It sounded as if someone had jumped onto the metal floor of the fire escape.

She held her breath. Nothing. Exhaling with relief, Nancy pushed open the bathroom door the same second a black shape hurtled through the bedroom window.

Glass flew everywhere. Nancy ducked her head and threw her arms over her face. Then she heard a sinister chuckle, and her breath caught in her throat. Framed in the light of the broken window was the ski-masked attacker from the alley!

Swiftly, the person pulled out a knife. With a cry, Nancy jumped backward. The knife slashed through the air as she crashed into the doorjamb.

Whoever it is must think I'm Rachel! Nancy realized in horror.

She ripped off the red wig. The black figure paused for a second, giving Nancy just enough time to make a dash for the door to the hallway.

But the figure in black got to the door ahead of her and blocked it. Glancing around for a weapon, Nancy grabbed a lamp from a small nightstand and held it in front of her.

"Don't come any closer," she warned.

The attacker chuckled. "Always on top of things, right, Ms. Drew? Only this time, I'm afraid you made a big mistake and had the wrong person arrested."

Reaching up, the person plucked off the ski mask.

Nancy inhaled sharply.

It was Mr. A!

Chapter

Sixteen

THE DIRECTOR of the teen center gave Nancy a
sinister smile.

"So I was right," Nancy said breathlessly.
"Mrs. Thackett didn't kill Paul."

"Which is why I need to get rid of you." Mr.
A's cheeks were flushed, and his bald head glis-
tened with sweat. Nancy couldn't believe the
mild-mannered director was the person who'd
attacked her in the alley.

His eyes narrowed. "I figured once you got
hold of the page from the account ledger, you'd
figure it out. That's why you're more dangerous
than Rachel. I only wish I'd killed you last night
in the alley."

Nancy clutched the lamp tightly. "So you knew
I was onto you?"

He nodded. "I knew it wouldn't be long. Then

140

dear Mrs. Johnson called this morning about another donation. She mentioned how thoughtful it had been for someone from the center to call thanking her for February's donation. When I asked her who had called, she mentioned you."

As if to emphasize his point, he thrust the knife blade closer. Nancy's gaze flickered from the blade to Mr. A's eyes. Anger gleamed in them. How had he been able to hide his true side all this time?

"Well, that cleared up two things," he continued, his voice low. "One, I finally figured out what else Paul had put in that envelope besides the account page he stole from the ledger. He stuck that check in, hoping that whoever got it would put two and two together."

"And come up with the fact that you've been embezzling funds from the teen center," Nancy finished for him.

He shrugged. "You look at it as embezzlement. I look at it as payment for services rendered. After all, who else would have worked so hard for a bunch of high-school dropouts? And it was the perfect setup, too, until Paul started checking out my account ledger. He thought he was doing me a favor. After a couple of business courses, he figured he could help me straighten out my books."

Mr. A snorted disdainfully. "When I found out what he was doing, I put the ledger in a locked file drawer. But I was too late; Paul had already noticed the center was taking in more money than it spent. When he asked me about it, I told him the money was in a special account for the new dorm."

"And he believed you?"

"Until the little crook broke into the file drawer and found my account book."

"From Chicago Bank and Trust."

Mr. A looked sharply at Nancy. "How'd you know about that?" he growled, his gloved hand tensing on the knife.

Nancy took a step backward, bumping her hip into the nightstand. She steadied the lamp in her hand, in case the director was ready to spring.

"Paul again, huh." Mr. A's eyes narrowed.

"So how did you actually embezzle the money?" Nancy asked, trying to keep her voice steady. "You must have deposited any donations that didn't require a receipt in the J. R. Communications account, right?"

"Something like that. You'd be surprised how many do-gooders out there donate anonymously. All they want in return is for me to call and tell them how wonderful they are. It was a perfect setup until that senile Mrs. Johnson brought her February check over and gave it to Paul instead of me. She must've told him about all her contributions to the center."

Nancy shifted her weight so that she was slightly closer to the door. If she could only distract him somehow, she could escape. "Of course," Nancy said calmly, "Paul was smart enough to notice that her donations weren't recorded in the ledger and realize that you were putting them in your own account under a false name."

"The lady gets a prize!" Mr. A sniggered. "He said he wanted to meet Monday night. When I told him it had to be away from the center, he suggested behind the warehouse by the tracks—his turf, he called it." Mr. A's chuckle was low and evil, and Nancy shivered, repulsed by him.

"When we met and Paul confronted me about everything he'd found out, I figured he was going to blackmail me. Was I in for a big surprise! Mr. ex-Nighthawk had turned into a do-gooder. He said he'd keep all the information in an envelope and put it in a safe place with instructions that if something happened to him, the envelope was to go to the police. He told me that he'd destroy it if I gave back all the money to the center and resigned. Otherwise, he was going to the police himself." Mr. A shook his head slowly. "I tried to reason with him, even offered to cut him in on the deal, but he was too stubborn. So I killed him."

He said it so coldly that Nancy instinctively gripped the lamp tighter. It was her only protection from this madman. "So that's why you were after Rachel and ransacked her apartment? You figured she had the envelope?"

"That's right, Ms. Drew," he replied.

"And that's why you showed up in the alley last night?"

He nodded. "I planned on getting there early and just grabbing the envelope. But Rachel didn't show up until right before you did—"

"And to get the evidence, you had to get rid of me. Only my friends stopped you," Nancy finished for him.

"And now I think you're stalling," he said, "hoping one of those lamebrain cops I sneaked by will come to your rescue. Only when they finally do get up here, you're going to be dead." Waving his knife, he gestured toward the window. "Climb out on that fire escape. You're going to have a bad fall."

"This is crazy! The cops are right out front. You won't be able to get away with this." Nancy yanked the cord from the wall, then swung the lamp in front of her like a club.

Mr. A jumped backward. "Oh, but I will." He gave her another sick grin. "I'll ditch the black outfit and walk right past them. The cops aren't looking for a short, skinny, bald guy. And if they do stop me, I'll tell them I'm here to see Detective Hawkins about some important information."

Nancy flushed. He was right. If she didn't stop him, he just might get away with it.

Using the lamp like a sword, Nancy thrust it at the director's hand. The shade caught the blade of the knife. It flew from his grasp and went skittering across the floor, toward the door.

Nancy dove after it. Her fingers wrapped around the handle. At the same time, Mr. A dropped to the floor, and his gloved hand grabbed hers.

He squeezed Nancy's fingers. Tears stung her eyes. Drawing up one leg, she kicked sideways with all her might.

She could feel her foot connect with muscle, and the man grunted with pain. Then strong fingers reached for her throat. Nancy gasped for air. Letting go of the knife, she clawed at his fingers with both hands.

Just then a roar of anger came from above both of them. Suddenly Mr. A's hands were yanked from Nancy's throat. She coughed, then looked up.

B.D. had grabbed the man's shoulders. He picked Mr. A up and threw him against the wall. In an instant B.D. had drawn his gun and aimed it at Mr. A's head. "Make one move and I'll blow your brains out."

The director hesitated, then bowed his head.

B.D. glanced anxiously at Nancy. "Are you all right? You were up here so long that I got worried and decided to check on you."

Nancy took a ragged breath, then smiled. *"I'm glad you did. And now that we've really closed this case, I feel great!"*

* * *

Two days later George and Nancy stood in the lobby of the River Heights airport. In front of the security gates, Kyle and Bess were wrapped in a romantic embrace.

"Uh, how much longer are those two going to say goodbye?" George asked, glancing at her watch.

Nancy laughed. "Probably until Kyle's flight is announced," she said.

Just then the loudspeaker blasted, "Flight Eleven to Chicago is now boarding at Gate Twenty-two."

George breathed a sigh of relief. "Thank goodness. I was afraid we'd miss our hotline shift."

With one last kiss, Kyle and Bess parted. Kyle went through the security gate, waving at Bess until he was out of sight.

When Bess joined Nancy and George, she sighed deeply. Her eyes were red from crying, and her mascara had run down her cheeks.

Nancy handed her a tissue. Then she and George linked their arms with Bess's and escorted her from the airport.

"It's so sad." Bess sighed again. "Even though Kyle promised he'd write, I know it won't last. He's going to be so busy and—"

"You'll be busy, too," George said, patting her cousin's arm.

Bess's eyes brightened. "That's true. There's the hotline and my self-defense course—"

"And Tony," Nancy added teasingly.

Bess blushed. "Well, maybe. Hey. Isn't it almost dinnertime?" she asked, stopping abruptly. "I hope you two don't expect me to answer hotline calls on an empty stomach."

"No, we'll stop for a bite to eat first," Nancy said, winking at George.

"It's good to hear you're thinking about food again, Bess," George added. "That must mean you're going to be all right!"

An hour later Nancy, Bess, and George walked into the hotline office. Billie and Rachel were answering the phones. When she saw Nancy, Rachel jumped up and greeted her with a big hug.

"I didn't expect to see you here so soon," Nancy said. Rachel grinned happily. "Hey. The hotline saved my life," Rachel replied. "I owe it lots of volunteer hours. I'm just observing now, but pretty soon I'll be taking calls with the best of you."

George, Bess, and Nancy laughed. Billie was hanging back by the desk.

"And, Nancy, my mom owes you her life," Rachel added. "The police are only going to charge her with fleeing the scene of the crime and obstructing an investigation."

"What was she doing at the warehouse?" Nancy asked.

Rachel rolled her eyes. "Following Paul. That same night, the private eye she hired had tailed Paul to my apartment. He called my mom, and she stormed over to confront him again. Remember, she'd 'paid' him off. When she arrived, he was leaving to meet Mr. A. She followed. She saw him drive to the back of the warehouse, and she waited out front. When he didn't return, she decided to see where he had gone. By the time she got to the tracks, he was already dead."

Bess grimaced. "Could she be put in jail?"

"No." Rachel shook her head. "She's already hired some hotshot lawyer."

"And compared with Mr. A, she's really getting off light," Nancy said. "B.D. said they're racking up the evidence against him. The same knife he threatened me with is the murder weapon, his prints are all over the tape recorder in the basement, plus, they traced the J. R. Communications account to him."

"And then there's always his confession to you, Nan," Bess pointed out. "That should put him behind bars forever."

"Right. Most of the loose ends have been tied up, but I still have some questions." Nancy turned to Rachel. "Since it was Mr. A who bugged the phones, how did your mom find you at the hotel?"

"That detective she hired tracked me to the Chestmont about the same time the police did," Rachel answered. "That's why she burst into the room. She was expecting a joyful reunion." Rachel grimaced. "Fat chance of that."

"What *is* going to happen between you and your mom?" George asked.

Rachel sighed wearily, and her shoulders slumped. "I don't know. She's always run my life, but this escapade was the last straw." Her eyes filled with tears, and she sighed loudly.

"You all right?" Billie had silently come up beside Rachel. Nancy could tell by the concern in Billie's voice that the two were becoming good friends.

Nancy touched Rachel's arm gently. "Maybe all that happened will help her see she needs to make some changes."

"Talking about changes, who's going to take over running the center?" George asked.

"Me!"

The five girls swung their heads around. Tony was standing in the doorway of the office, a jubilant expression on his face.

"Tony! That's great!" everyone exclaimed, then started asking questions.

He held up his hands. "Slow down. There's still a lot to be worked out, but since I'm graduating in two months, I'll take over full-time this summer. Of course, the board of directors has suggested a few changes. For instance, the city will help fund the center from now on, which means I'll get a salary, and the financial side of things will be better policed."

"That's terrific, Tony," Bess said. "Should we start calling you Mr. R?"

Everyone laughed.

"No way. But I hope you guys will stick

around. The center's going to need lots of volunteers."

Nancy looked at the other girls. "I think we can handle it, right, guys?"

They all agreed. When they'd stopped chattering and laughing, Billie shyly glanced over at Nancy. "Before I go, I—we—need to thank you, too. Kip and the others, well, they're not much on thank-yous, and I know they aren't totally innocent, either," she added in a rush. "If Kip hadn't been involved with that robbery in the first place, no one would have even suspected him."

"Does he know that?" Nancy asked gently.

Billie shrugged. "Yeah. Fortunately, charges were dropped on that drugstore thing, and the whole murder scare really made him think about what he wants to do with the rest of his life."

She blushed as if embarrassed by her speech. Bending over, she pulled a jacket off the seat of the chair, then held it up. It was a black leather jacket with the letter *N* on the front.

"From us to you," Billie said.

"It's great!" Nancy exclaimed, taking it. "I love it. Hey! Did the gang give Mr. A a jacket, too?" she asked.

Billie nodded. "Yeah, about six months ago. To thank him for all the work he was doing for the kids in the neighborhood."

"So that's how he got one," Nancy murmured to herself, glad that one more piece of the puzzle had fallen into place. It was sad, though, she thought, that a man who had done so much good should end up being so evil.

"Try it on," Bess said, interrupting Nancy's pensive thoughts.

Nancy smiled as she slipped on the jacket. It fit perfectly.

"To Nancy Drew," Billie said, grinning. "From all the members of the Nighthawks. Thanks for finding out who really killed Paul Remer!"

Nancy's next case:

Nancy has come to Riverfront amusement park at the invitation of famed illusionist Adriana Polidori. Having inherited the park after her uncle's tragic death, Adriana now finds herself on a roller-coaster ride of terror. For Riverfront has suddenly been transformed into a world of delusion, deception, and potential disaster!

The danger begins with the sabotage of Adriana's magic act and quickly spreads throughout the complex. Squeals of joy turn to shrieks of fear as the park's rides spin out of control. To rescue Riverfront, Nancy knows she'll have to work some magic of her own. A dirty trickster is on the loose, bent on making Adriana disappear . . . permanently . . . in *Illusions of Evil,* Case #94 in The Nancy Drew Files™.